RUNNING IN FLIP-FLOPS FROM THE END OF THE WORLD

RUNNING IN FLIP-FLOPS FROM THE END OF THE WORLD

justin a. reynolds

Scholastic Inc.

ISBN 978-1-339-05376-9

10 9 8 7 6 5 4 3 2 1   24 25 26 27 28

Printed in the U.S.A. 40

Published in hardcover by Scholastic Press, April 2024

This edition first printing, January 2024

Book design by Stephanie Yang

For every foot who's ever had to
"run" in flip-flops, I feel your pain.

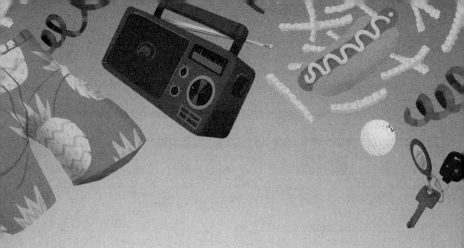

An extremely brief but super necessary opening note from your friendly narrator and master storyteller, Eddie Gordon Holloway:

I know, I know, I owe you a **MAJOR** apology for the way things ended last time.

Um, yeah, ya do! A cliff-hanger, Eddie, for real? Man, I thought we were friends.

We are friends! Good friends!

Hmph. Are we? Because news flash, Eddie, there are two things friends don't leave friends on. On read or on cliff-hangers, okay? That's Basic Friendship 101, dude.

I hear you. You're absolutely right.

Of course we are.

But the truth is, I didn't have much of a choice.

But hold on, aren't you narrating this story?

It's complicated. Am I the main narrator here? Yes. But do I have final say on *how* the story's told? Nope. See, there are a lot of factors, um, factoring in . . . and well, all I can say is, if you please give me another chance, I promise I'll prove to you I still got you, same as before, same as always, yeah?

SIGH. Okay, Eddie, yes—

YESSS!! SWEET!! This is so exciting, you guys have no idea—

But, Eddie, we're serious, you've gotta do better.

Hey, say less. I'm gonna *do better* better than better's ever been done in the history of do-bettering!

Why do we get the feeling we're gonna regret this?

Hahaha, guys, staaaahhp. Trust me! I *still* got you!

An equally if not briefer but still just as necessary second opening note from your friendly narrator and master story-teller, Eddie Gordon Holloway:

Okay, so now that we're back to being great friends again, can I just say how STOOPID HAPPY and DUMB EXCITED I am to see you?! Like, I really mean it. Big thanks, from the heart, for showing up for me again. I can't explain how much it means to me.

No, seriously, last time we were together things got pretty hairy in a hurry, what with every single person in our town of Carterville, Ohio, including all our family and friends, going to the shore for Beach Bash, aka The Best Party of the Entire Year, only to never return home again.

No, you heard me right.

There's no one left.

Every single person in our hometown has:

Gone missing.

Vanished without a trace.

Disappeared.

Evaporated into thin air.

Been abducted by smelly aliens, teleported to a galaxy far, far away, and forced to spend every waking hour of every day hand-popping alien back pimples—which is 100 percent as gross as it sounds. Especially because no matter how much the people complain, they can't wear gloves. Nope, all that zit bursting is bare-hand action only. Although, in fairness, this is not because the aliens are completely ruthless, uncaring meanies—no, when they came to Earth to take humans, they forgot to grab disposable gloves and, unfortunately, while they do happen to have a large supply of gloves back on their alien home planet, they have seventeen zigzagging alien fingers per hand *and* each of their alien hands is roughly the size of a garbage truck, so the humans couldn't use alien gloves even if they wanted to.

And I know what you're thinking—*Eddie, if the aliens' hands are as big as garbage trucks, how humongous are their back pimples?!*

I don't wanna make you guys nauseous but let's just say, on average, it takes one human sixteen days, nine hours, and forty-seven

4

seconds to pop ONE alien pimple. And the fluid from each alien pimple is enough to fill 137 normal-sized swimming pools . . . so, how big are they? You be the judge.

You're still thinking about alien zits, aren't you?

Okay, yes, maybe I got a little carried away with that last bit. I mean, odds are they probably *weren't* kidnapped by pimply, stinky aliens. But really, we have zero clue where they are. All we know is it's been two days since we suddenly found ourselves 100 percent alone and entirely on our own without our family or friends.

I'm not sure I ever mentioned this—even if I did, it deserves another nod, because it's *that* important—but I 100 percent appreciate you being there with us, for rocking with us from the beginning to the end (of part one, haha).

For real for real.

Definitely pat yourself on the back with both hands—yep, The Double-Pat—because you're a real one!

I mean, not everyone would go along for the ride with me and the crew the way you did. You didn't ask any questions. Okay, well, when you did ask questions, they were really good ones. Plus, you didn't complain. You just showed up and balled out and I know that took real guts, a big heart, and—as Mom likes to say—*strength of character.* For real, you rock! And well, I just hope you know, as far as Xavier, Sage, Trey, Sonia, and myself are concerned, you aren't just along for the ride. Nope, you are also a valuable member of this team. Basically, you're one of us now. And that means we ride together, no matter what, now and always.

So, hop in, friend—we've got places to go and, hopefully, if we're lucky, *people* to see!

5400

Question: Is there any smell better than summer?

Answer: No. No, there is not.

I'm right where we left off last time, in the driver's seat of Wanna-Be Dad's precious car, about to head to the beach to look for clues about what happened to our families. I roll down the windows, the cool summer morning breeze rolling in, tickling the hairs on my arm, whistling gently in my ear.

Seriously, if laundry detergent smelled as good as summer, I'd feel better about risking my life going into our creepy basement.

But, Eddie, there IS detergent that smells like summer. The scent is actually called Summer Breeze. So, see, now maybe you can do some laundry and maybe, you know, get out of the bathing suit you've been wearing this whole time?

Gee, thanks so much, guys. That's really super helpful. I'll get right on that, as soon as I finish scuba diving on Jupiter.

Huh? But you're not scuba diving on . . . Ohhh. You're being sarcastic.

I'm sorry, but really, you left me no choice.

But also, I have a confession to make. The opening lines you just read? They weren't fully true. I know, I know, withholding the real story is not the best way to kick our reunion off, but the thing is, the truth is so awful and seeing how we only just now got back together, I dunno, I guess I wanted to start things off on a positive note, know what I mean?

But okay, you're right. The truth is always the best option.

So here's an idea. How 'bout we start this thing over, this time with the truth, the whole truth, and nothing but the truth? Y'all good with that? And might y'all find it in your beautiful, forgiving hearts to kindly accept my sincerest apology, along with my promise to tell you guys exactly how things are, no matter how ugly and depressing?

Wait, what's that?

You wanna know *just how ugly and depressing we're talking about*?

Well, I think I've already said too much, so how about I let you guys decide for yourselves?

Okay, cool, whenever you're ready, go ahead and turn the page and we'll get on with The Truth about How Things Actually Are, yeah?

And, guys, good luck out there.

You're gonna need it.

THE REAL 5400

First of all, I'm super hot.

No, wait! Not how you think!

I mean, not how I *think* you're thinking. Obvi, you could be thinking something totally different . . .

Say, uh, real quick, just for kicks and giggles, which way *are* you thinking?

Like is it more, *Okay, Eddie play too much, but he is lowkey kinda cute, though*—or are you more, *Ugh, the only thing hot about Eddie is his mouth, 'cause he mad thirsty?*

Wait! No! Never mind, I don't wanna know.

Unless you wanna tell me. Don't let me stop you.

an awkward silence washes over us

Sigh. Why am I like this, y'all?

M'kay, welp, y'all good with a redo? Cool, cool, cool.

Summer Sucks, Take 2? 3? Whatever. Let's just do this already.

Okay, from the top, in five . . . four . . . three . . . two . . .

~~~~~

First of all, I'm super hot.

No, not how you think. Yes, I'm cute, but I'm talking temperature. It's hotter than two bushy squirrels fighting for a walnut in a wool sock.

I roll down all four windows, expecting a cool morning breeze to rush in, insta-chilling our damp foreheads, our perspiring armpits, and our sweat-soaked backs.

Sike. I'm playing, there are ZERO COOL BREEZES happening.

Instead, there's a ginormous gust of RIDICULOUSLY HOT AIR blowing right at us.

I roll the windows back up. I tried to be environmentally conscious—save the turtles and all that—but it's dumb hot outside. I smash the air conditioner button. Ahh, yes, that's better already.

I push my cool sunglasses back up my nose and scan the car, making sure I look everyone dead in their eyes—

"You guys feel that?" I ask.

Trey shakes his head. "Feel what?"

"The only thing I feel is hot," Xavier whines.

I ignore him because this is no time for negativity. "That, my friends, is the feeling of hope rippling through the air."

Sage smiles. "I feel it."

"Me too," Sonia says.

I grin. "You guys ready to rock and roll?"

Everyone nods, except Xavier. "As long as rock 'n' roll doesn't involve driving the car into a tree, then yes, let's go."

"Ha. No promises," I say with a wink as I turn back toward the steering wheel. "Someone count me down from three."

Trey laughs. "Three . . ."

"Two," Sonia chimes.

"One!" Sage shouts.

I mash the gas pedal and the car jerks but stays in place.

"Wait, what's going on?" I ask aloud.

Sonia reaches across the front seat and taps the shifter. "You're gonna wanna shift outta park and into reverse."

I laugh nervously as beads of sweat roll down my face. "Duh. Just testing your copilot skills and, ta-da, you passed!"

Sonia rolls her eyes. "Mhm."

I shift the car into reverse. "Second time's the charm."

I press my flip-flop against the gas pedal and this time— surprise—WBD's car rolls backward. We're officially rolling—which *whew*. Not gonna lie, outside I'm the picture of cool, calm, and casual—but inside? *Bruh*. Inside, I'm mad relieved. Yeah, this is only step one in GET TO THE BEACH TO LOOK FOR CLUES ABOUT WHERE EVERYONE WENT, but imagine if we didn't even make it out the driveway. Talk about a vibe killer.

Except a few seconds later we're out of my driveway and on the street, and everyone celebrates with clapping and *whoop whoops*. I seat dance a little.

Thirty seconds more and we're cruising down Ellison Avenue, the pink penguins decorating my front lawn shrinking in the rearview mirror. And who knows—maybe this'll be easier than we thought. I've been driving barely two minutes and already the steering wheel feels at home in my hands, like I've been doing this for years. Meanwhile, my mega-annoying older brother—aka The Bronster—failed his driving test THREE TIMES, ha. Guess I'm a natural.

Also, I assumed driving sucked because Mom's constantly complaining about driving me around—but, um, wrong! Driving's dope! And easy! Seriously, the fact you gotta be sixteen to legally drive is bananas. Ha, add it to the How We Know Adults Hate Kids Having Fun list. I mean, I'm nowhere near sixteen and look, no hands—

"Boy, if you don't put your hands back on that wheel," Sonia snaps.

I retake the wheel and toss her a wink. "Don't worry. I got this."

"Eddie, look out!" Sage yells from the back seat.

And at first I don't see anything, but then something flashes into the middle of the road.

"Eddie, turn! Turn! You're gonna hit—" Sonia starts, but doesn't finish her sentence because instead she gets the really bright idea to take control of the wheel herself. Except between her hands turning the wheel right, and mine angling left, our path doesn't change a bit.

Nope, in fact, we're only seconds away from crashing into . . . whatever that thing is.

"Sonia, let go!" I yell. "You're gonna get us killed!"

And I see the fear in her eyes as she lets go and drops back into her seat. I quickly jerk the wheel left, knowing that with a little bit of luck there's still a good chance we don't hit it—

BOOM!

THUMP!

THUD!

5500

The car leaps into the air, and for a second, we're flying, as whatever we hit ricochets beneath us like the world's unluckiest pinball.

PLINK! PLUKE! POINK PLUNK PLICK PLINK PONK!

But that's nothing compared to what we hear next.

Aka The Worst Sound Ever—*SCRRRRRZZZZPPPPRTTTXXX.*

As in, not only did we just hit an unidentified object, it's still stuck under the car, which means currently we're dragging it clear down the street.

And out of nowhere, the bright morning sky's gone, the sun swarmed by dark purple clouds. Above us, yellow-white lightning flashes, karate-chopping the horizon in half like it's a rotted two-by-four. A few raindrops smack the windshield. Then a few handfuls splash across the car hood, and before you know it, buckets of rainwater thump into the glass like we're a ship in a sea storm, the windshield wipers going bonkers keeping up, thrashing left and right.

Great, it's one thing to drive your stepdad's most prized possession in perfect weather, but in rain heavy enough to drown a desert?

"Stop the car, Eddie!" Trey yells, his long neck twisting like when you wring out a beach towel. He's staring out the back window. "I think . . . something's trapped under the car."

"Don't stop! What if it's in a weird position? Stopping might make it worse," Sage argues. "Stick to the mission. We'll check after we make it to the beach."

But Trey's not buying it. "What if it's a person? Or an animal?"

I shake my head. "It wasn't alive, guys. It was probably trash."

But Trey won't be denied. "Stop the car, Eddie! Now!"

"Fine," I say with a sigh. "Better hold on." I smash the brakes and the tires squeal in the rain as the back of the car fishtails wildly left, then right, before lurching forward with enough speed and velocity to nearly throw us from our seats. Xavier gets the worst of it, both of his knees smacking into the middle thingie dividing the two front seats.

I put the car in park, but I don't turn it off. "Everyone okay?"

Xavier massages his kneecaps. "Yeah, it's not like I need knees," he groans.

If my mom was driving, she'd 100 percent use this moment to emphasize how wearing seat belts save lives.

MOM: *Let me tell you about the time somebody I knew a long time ago, when I was about your age, had a truly terrible thing happen to them all because they weren't being safe. Because they chose having fun and looking cool over protecting themselves. And now guess where they are?*

ME: *Umm, at an amusement park having the time of their life?*

MOM: *No, Eddie. They're dead!*

ME: *Hmm. We're sure they're not on a roller coaster?*

"Anyone else hurt?" I ask, looking at everyone to make sure. And that's when I see it in their eyes. Fear and horror. I wonder if they see the same in mine.

"What . . . was that?" Sage asks.

"A deer?" Xavier says.

Trey shakes his head. "My dad hit a deer once and his entire car was wrecked. If we hit a deer, we'd know it."

Sonia turns toward me. "You're quiet, Eddie. What do you think we hit?"

I scrunch my face. "There are three other people in this car, how come you're asking me?"

Sonia looks at me the same way your teacher looks at you when she's passing out a pop quiz and you ask if it's open book. "Because you're driving."

I shrug. "What? You for real think just 'cause I'm driving, I'm gonna know when I run something over?"

Sonia looks even more confused now. "Yes."

"Well, don't worry. It was probably just a bump in the road. Everything's fine."

Sonia folds her arms across her chest. "Before, you said it was trash."

"Did I?" I say, my voice squeaking a bit.

"Maybe one of us should get out and check," Sage offers.

"Yeah, but who?" Xavier adds.

Everyone's eyes instantly shift toward me, like eight big spotlights. At first I ignore them, keeping my head turned and my eyes out my window, rather than giving in to their bossy eyes.

But then Xavier's all, "Eddie should check."

Which, with best friends like X, who needs enemies? I twist around in my seat and it takes everything inside me not to hit him with The Most Evil Eye Ever. Instead, by some miracle, I force out a fake smile and through clenched teeth I manage a not-very-convincing "Gee, thanks, *friend*."

Xavier shrugs. "Bro, this whole *let's get in my stepdad's car and drive to the beach plan* was your bright idea, remember?"

"Whatever, dude," I say, my hand already reaching for my door handle, my fingers wrapping around the lever, the same lever that'll unlock and open only my car door, and officially designate me as The Kid Who Will Investigate What the Car Might've Run Over.

And I know what you're thinking. *Eddie, why are you so afraid to check?*

Except that's where you're wrong. I'm not scared. I'm just . . . cautious. What if it's some alien goblin pretending it's hurt so it can eat my brains? Or what if it's a mutant chipmunk and it karate chops me in the throat?

Eddie, what are the odds?

Which is a fair question . . . if it was two days ago when life was normal, when I couldn't wait for Saturday and the Beach Bash, back when I was literally drooling at the prospect of sinking my jumbo straw deep in an extra-large Triple Berry Tongue Slap Your Brain Stupid Silly Super Slushie.

Now everything's screwed up.

Now anything's possible. Even mutant, karate-chopping *rodentia* (fancy word for chipmunks = rodents).

So, no, I'm not afraid. But also, would it be so strange if I was?

I start to pull the lever. Everyone's watching me, waiting for me to make a move.

I could just *not* get out.

Maybe if I stall a bit, someone tires of waiting and hops out?

But judging by their *Eddie, don't even look my way* expressions, I'm pretty sure no one's gonna volunteer as tribute and take the potential L for me. Nope, this is all me.

And here's the thing my brain won't let go of: If the five of us had gone to Beach Bash, like we were supposed to, where would we be right now?

With our family and friends, that's where.

I pull the lever and climb outside into the pouring rain.

5600

When I first peek under WBD's car, I'm technically looking, though admittedly, maybe not in the traditional way one "looks."

As you're likely aware, there are levels to "looking."

There's STRATEGIC LOOKING, or *STROOKING*, a logic-based approach that focuses on eliminating impossibilities.

For example, say you're looking for *xylophone* in a word search; you're not paying attention to *g*'s or *w*'s or *c*'s, right? Nope, you're locked in on all the *x*'s because why waste time looking at impossible solutions?

Then there's *MOOKING*, better known as *MOM LOOKING*.

Like when you can't find a thing even though you've searched everywhere and your mom's insisting *It's in the bathroom under the sink next to your dandruff shampoo* and you're all, *Nope, I already looked there*, and she shoots back, *But did you look GOOD, because I know it's there*, and you're like, *It's NOT there, I double-checked*, so now she's all irritated like, *It IS there and if I come find it where I'm telling you to look, you're gonna be in trouble*—and you roll your eyes hard because, ugh, how dare she suggest you don't know how to look good, as if looking is some special skill you've gotta go to school for, but you look again anyway and you can't wait to holler back *Nope, still not there*, except somehow it is there, exactly where she said, and you're mad salty—and you try to tiptoe back to your room without saying anything because the last thing you wanna hear is her going off about being right, but it's too late, she appears in front of you like magic, her lips pursed like, *Mmhm, that's what I thought, I knew you didn't look GOOD*, and you're all, *Actually, it was kinda* behind *my dandruff shampoo, but go off.* Except that last sentence you only say in your head because you'd like to make it to high school.

So, yeah, I'm *looking* but maybe not how *you'd* look, know what I mean?

My eyes aren't what you'd call 100 percent open.

I'm kinda sorta squinting.

And by squinting, I mean if you tapped on your phone's flashlight and shone it directly at my face, only a sliver of light would squeeze into my eyes.

And by sliver, I mean zero. As in zero slivers of light will sneak into my eye sockets. As in there's a better chance of you opening your palm right now and finding a one-hundred-dollar bill than any light shining into my eyeballs.

Which is why, when I drop to my knees and poke my head under the car, I see:

"Nothing. I don't see anything," I shout up to the others, shining a flashlight I found in WBD's glove compartment from the front tires to the back. I'm about to stand up and make a show of brushing gravel and dirt off my shirt and knees, because—pro tip: Dusting yourself off is always a sign of hard work—when suddenly a voice from the other side of the car exposes me.

"Eddie, your eyes are closed, bro."

And without thinking, my eyes pop open quickly, and there, on the other side of the car, staring back at me? Xavier's *when the power went out I was in the middle of cutting my own hair so now I'm stuck with half-a-fro* butt. Then Sage's pigtails drop into view as her head joins Xavier's. Really, now everybody wants to look? Where was this enthusiasm two minutes ago?

"No, I had something in my eyes, I was trying to squeeze it out," I say.

But, Eddie, why didn't you just admit you were afraid to look? Your friends would understand, no?

Probably, but what can I say?—I'm a human. We're complicated creatures.

"Well, I can't believe what I'm seeing under here," Xavier says, his eyes sweeping back and forth across the bit of pavement beneath the car. "Nope, I can't stinking believe it."

And I was so worried about being exposed as a coward I'd opened my eyes, yes, but I'd only aimed them at Xavier. But now, I let them follow Xavier's gaze, zeroed right in on the back of the car, where he was staring with his face twisted in confusion.

And what I see there, well, Xavier already put it best:

I can't stinking believe it.

5700

There's nothing. Nada. Zip. Zilch.

No blood. No fur or feathers. No shiny robot guts or gooey alien slime.

Not the slightest shred of evidence that we'd hit anything.

Xavier and his mooking behind can't find a trace, either, even though he practically crawls around the car, inspecting every inch like he's on a treasure hunt . . . all this in the middle of a torrential downpour. Seriously, he's so soaked in rain, his half-fro's beginning to droop. Dude even asks Trey to boost him up so he can see the roof, which Trey politely declines because *duh, while we may disagree on whether we hit something, we fully agree nothing came close to the roof.*

In fact, every part of the car, including the chrome underbody, is practically gleaming, which is no surprise, considering the disproportionate hours WBD spends washing, waxing, and detailing versus the hours he actually drives the car. Seriously, we've gotta be talking a 6:1 ratio. I'm not exaggerating—for every hour WBD allows himself the pleasure of zipping this baby along real roads, he spends six-ish hours making it sparkle like new.

Wow, Eddie. Sounds like WBD's cheating himself outta a lot of fun!

I know, right?! I almost sorta feel bad for the guy.

Meanwhile, back at the non-crime scene, X, Sage, and I retrace our path back fifty-plus feet, searching for any signs of a collision, any clues, but nope, nothing on, or on the side of, the road. Plus, after careful inspection and to my unexplainable relief, there's not even a scratch on the front bumper.

"I don't see anything," I yell over a blast of thunder. "Should we head back to the car?"

"Huh?" Sage yells back.

I try again—"Should we head back to the car?"—but of course, the thunder decides to erupt as soon as I open my mouth, making it impossible to hear me.

The thunder stops. "We can't hear you," X says, pointing to his ears. "What did you say?"

Ha, if the thunder thinks it's gonna get me again, it's got another thing coming—this time I open my mouth and pause—and sure enough the thunder booms like a cannon. I wait for it to stop and then I finally get the words out. "Sorry, the thunder kept covering over my voice. What I said was, 'I don't—'"

The deafening thunder claps across the sky.

Okay, I give up.

"I don't see anything," Sage says.

"Agreed. Should we head back to the car?" X suggests.

"Yes, great idea," Sage replies.

"Actually, I was the one who—"

Another blast of thunder rocks our eardrums. Okay, now this feels personal. Why is it that whenever I try and talk, it—

"Eddie, what are you doing?" X calls to me, because apparently he and Sage have already started running to the car.

"We should probably hurry," Sage adds.

And I'm tempted to be in my feelings over the thunderous interruptions, but instead I chase after my friends feeling happy and vindicated—because at the end of the day, I was . . . I was . . .

Wait, what's the word? What's the . . .

I was r-r-r . . .

Oh, yeah, I was RIGHT. R-I-G-H-T. RIGHT! RIGHT! RIGHT! HAHAHAHAHA!

So yep, my smile is on 10 as I triumphantly sliiiiide into the driver's seat. Well, more like I scoot, then scoot some more, then scoot again—apparently when you're soaking wet your butt doesn't slide across leather seats as easily as you might think.

"Nope, Eddie," Sonia says, eyeing me from the passenger seat as she rebuckles her seat belt. "Don't you dare. Don't you dare say—"

"Say what?" I say with an innocent smile. "Ohhh, you mean, *I told ya so*," I add, hitting her with a wink so exaggerated it almost makes me dizzy.

"Yeah, yeah, fine. But we *know* we hit something. We all heard it," Sonia insists. The others echo their agreement.

My smile pauses its takeover of my face. "Okay, then, assuming you all are right, then where does that leave us?"

Sonia's eyes sharpen and her forehead scrunches together like an accordion; this is her *give me a sec, I'm in deep thought* mode. "If we're right and we did hit something, then that raises two important questions. The first we already know. *What* did we hit?" Sonia pauses and turns to stare out her window.

"And the second question?" Trey prompts from the back seat.

Sonia gulps hard. "And where did it go?"

A thick, heavy silence falls over the car, like when you unfurl your fresh-from-the-dryer comforter in the air, blanketing your bed. We're so quiet, I swear I hear all five of our hearts racing.

Finally, Trey clears his throat. "Guys, there's one more question I can't shake," he says, leaning forward in his seat. "How come everything in this town keeps disappearing?"

5800

We're pretty shaken, so we decide Operation: Get to the Beach Now can wait.

Most of us, anyway.

We're piled back in the car and I'm about to attempt my first U-turn, when we realize someone's missing.

"Wait, where's my sister?" Trey asks, hand already reopening his door.

"Huh? She was here a second ago," I say, twisting to get a good look at the back seat, as if she's chilling back there and Xavier and Trey somehow missed her. Yep, it makes zero sense, but I look, anyway. It's like when you tell your friend, *I'm going to the store* and they immediately ask, *You're going to the store?* It's instincts, I guess.

"Dude, what are you doing?" Xavier asks, his face screwed up, clearly offended I'm double-checking the back seat. Which, again,

I get—do I really think he and Trey are straight up not seeing an entire human being in the back seat of an average-sized car? Nope, that's highly unlikely—but it's one of those things, you've gotta see for yourself, you feel better that way, you know? "Really? You think she's hiding under our feet? You don't think me and Trey can count to three?"

I shake my head. "Bro, I'm only making sure we—"

But before I get out my explanation, Trey explodes out the car the way he explodes through the paint during games, knifing to the hoop for a dizzying reverse layup. Except this time Trey doesn't stop exploding, this time he keeps running, sprinting through the wet grass in the still-pouring rain right toward the woods.

"Okay, now where's Trey going?" I ask, glancing at Sonia for support—Sonia, the definition of *cool and calm under pressure*, and my only other friend on the same level as Xavier.

"I don't know, but we should stick together," Xavier says.

Sonia hops out the car and chases after Trey.

"Or we could all get back out of the car," Xavier says. "That's an option, too. Except what if Sage comes back and we're all gone, so then she goes looking for us, but we're on our way back to the car, and it's just this vicious cycle of coming and going but never finding each other. It makes sense that Trey goes to look, but you and I should probably stay here, just in case Sage—"

I pop open my door and now I'm trailing after Sonia, who's chasing Trey, who's probably going after Sage. And all I can think is this:

1. I hope Sage is okay. Because what if whatever was on the road, the thing we hit, has her? What if, like everyone else in Carterville, Sage disappears now, too?
2. If there's one place in the entire town that I'd do anything to avoid, it's the spot just ahead, the spot Trey is currently racing right toward—

Witch Woods.

5900

You're wondering why's it called Witch Woods, right?

And if you're like me, the first time you heard someone say *Witch Woods*, your immediate response was *I don't know, which woods what?*

Anyway, I won't bore you with legend and folklore, but here's a hint: *This is not your new-age, fun, hippy aunt who's young enough to be your sister, doesn't believe in shoes because feet are obviously happier when they're free (and apparently dirty-ish), and who says she's only a witch in the sense that she really loves nature, weekend gardening, and casting the occasional happy spell in the forest with her closest animal friends* woods.

Nope, this is not Good Witch Woods.

Or even Green Witch Woods.

By age ten, if you haven't been warned away from Witch Woods a gazillion times, you need better friends—people don't love you.

Here's all you need to know (at least for now) about Witch Woods:

They're extra creepy.

Weird, unexplainable things happen inside them.

You should absolutely avoid them at all costs.

Oh, and apparently, years ago, a few kids ran into Witch Woods and, um, you know, were never heard from ever again. So, there's that, too.

6000

"Guys," I yell. "The woods, we're not supposed to—Maybe we shouldn't—"

But if Trey hears me, he doesn't waste time answering. I watch as Trey, with zero hesitation, disappears into the tall trees.

Without breaking stride, Sonia glances back at me. "You good?"

"I'm right behind you."

"It's gonna be okay," she says back, and I know she's remembering all the stories running through my head, all the reasons why Witch Woods is super off-limits. And Sonia's face twists like she might say more, but then she's gone, slipping into the woods.

A moment later, it's my turn. I shake my head, take a deep breath, and break the rule I've heard since second grade—I enter Witch Woods.

6100

A few feet into Witch Woods, all my friends *poof* into thin air.

I'm not sure if I'm suddenly running slower, or if Sage, Trey, and Sonia are suddenly running faster, but I'm barely into the trees and the other three are gone, baby, gone.

If not for this path of freshly trampled grass, I'd doubt they'd gone this way.

I glance back over my shoulder, kinda wishing Xavier will be there, jogging after me, a sheepish *haha, I changed my mind* look on his face, but nah—only thing running behind me is my own shadow.

I think you guys know by now, I'm no scaredy-cat. In fact, dare I say I'm pretty lowkey fearless sometimes—but, uh, random, unexpected jogs through creepy, dark woods? Not in my top five favorite exercises.

I run faster, hoping that'll help me catch up to them faster, but I still don't see them anywhere, and the woods only get darker and creepier.

I yell out, "Guys! Guys, where are you? Helllooooo?!"

And honestly, I'm not expecting anyone to answer me because, hello, I don't see anyone.

So . . . imagine my surprise . . . when I hear this:

"Eddie, is that you?" It sounds like Sonia and like she's right next to me, except there's no one actually there. I stop running and look all around me, trying my best to make out any humanlike shadows or shapes among the twisted trees and high grass, while also hoping that any humanlike shadows turn out to be, you know, humans . . . and, you know, humans that I *already know*.

"Sonia, is that you?" I ask back.

"Yeah, but how come I don't see you?"

I ask her the same question. But before she can answer, we hear:

"Eddie? Sonia? Is that really you or is my brain playing tricks on me?" Xavier asks.

Wait a minute. Xavier?! "X, I knew you'd come!" FOMO, making people do things they later regret since forever.

"Okay, so let me get this straight," Trey says. "No one can see anyone else right now, but we can all hear each other's voices?"

Yes, everyone agrees. Except how can that be? That's . . . impossible . . . right?

Yeah, it can't be a real thing. That doesn't make any sense, being able to hear my friends' voices but not see them? Not buying it. Something else is going on here and I have a feeling I know exactly what it is.

"Wait, you guys are playing a joke on me, right? Let me guess, you have a walkie-talkie hidden somewhere in the grass, right? And you guys are way back at the car, laughing at me, yeah? Or no, no, I got it. You're all hiding in the trees above me, right? That's it, isn't it? I figured it out."

But no one answers me for a solid fifteen seconds, which, given how fast my heart's currently beating, might as well be fifteen years!

"Eddie?" Sonia says.

"Yeah? What's up?" I say back.

"I thought your walkie-talkie theory was highly unlikely but at least not impossible . . ."

"Thank you," I say, only to realize she's not finished talking.

". . . But then you suggested we'd all climbed into these scary, gnarled trees and were somehow also projecting our voices right next to you, suggesting in addition to gaining incredible climbing skills in the last two minutes, we've also become expert ventriloquists capable of throwing our voices unbelievable distances."

I nod. "So you're saying I'm not *wrong* . . ."

Invisible Sonia laughs. "No, you're definitely wrong!"

"Okay, then, so how do you explain all this?"

"The same way we've explained everything else," X says. "We don't. It just . . . is."

"Okay, but there's gotta be a way to get back to each other, right? This can't be . . . permanent?!" I ask, not sure I want to know the answer and also knowing they won't have it, anyway.

And then Trey says, "Guys, we still have the same problem we started with."

Trey pauses—maybe for extra dramatic effect, or I don't know, maybe he just swallowed a weird flying bug—point is, no one else says a word, so I bite. "Which is?"

"Where's my sister?!"

6200

Where *is* Trey's sister? That's an excellent question and, as it turns out, we have our answer almost immediately.

"I'm over here!" a voice that sounds like Sage yells.

And even though I can't see anyone else, I think it's safe to assume we all do exactly the same thing at exactly the same time. We run toward Sage . . . well, her voice, anyway.

I follow her voice all the way back to the opening in the woods where we ran in—

And as I emerge, I'm startled to see Sonia, Trey, and Xavier all exit the woods at the same time as me. But that's not even the creepiest thing:

Somehow, we're all standing side by side!

As if we really were *with* each other in those woods, even though we couldn't actually see each other. And yeah, I have zero explanation for what just happened—I mean, I already gave you the walkie-talkie and tree-climbing theories, which were rather rudely shot down.

How about you guys figure this one out? Seriously, if you were ever gonna contribute to this story, now would be the time. Go ahead, lay your weirdest Witch Woods theories on me, I'll wait.

> *This space has been reserved for you to think of a theory. Please use this time wisely and not to grab a snack or fling cereal at your annoying sibling while you yell, "GET OUTTA MY ROOM."*
>
> *Thank you.*

And we're back.

And surprise! So is Sage, standing right beside the car, as if she'd never left.

Also, BREAKING NEWS: It turns out Sage wasn't just blindly running out into the scary woods just because.

"I was trying to get to the beach. I figured if we can't get there by car, then maybe I could get there by foot."

"You have any idea how long of a walk that is?" Xavier asks her.

She shakes her head. "No," she admits, softly. "How long?"

The four of us turn to Xavier for the answer and he smiles

sheepishly. "Why's everybody looking at me? I don't know, either. That's why I was asking."

The four of us groan because, c'mon, be for real, X.

"We can't just quit. We can't just give up," Sage insists.

But our minds are made up. "Who's quitting?" we shoot back, a little hurt she'd suggest we were, even though, in a way, we were.

"We'll try again later," I assure her.

"When the time's right," Sonia adds.

But Sage won't let it go. "What if our moms and dads are on that beach right now?" Sage argues, her voice high and tight, like when you really believe something, but no one's on your side.

Trey tries to comfort her the way I imagine cool big brothers do. I say *imagine* because my big brother, The Bronster? Dude's as cool and comforting as a frozen blankie in a snowstorm.

"Hey, we're not saying no," Trey explains. "We're just saying . . . right now's not the best time. I promise you we'll—"

"No! Now *is* the only time. It has to be now."

"Sage, I know you're worried about Mom and Dad. I . . . I am, too, but we have to start thinking about the big picture. They've been gone for days now. *Days.*"

I watch Sage's face drop a bit and I try to comfort her, try to think of how Real Dad, if he were still alive, would handle this. He always knew what to say. Always.

"Just because it's been days doesn't mean . . . it doesn't mean . . ."

Everyone stares at me, waiting for me to finish, to see what small morsel of hope I come up with to make us all feel at least a little better. And I rack my brain and a hundred things I could say fly in and out of it like, *Maybe we're on a new show called* Middle Grade Survivor, *and millions of people (including our parents) are watching to see if we'll find a way to hang on and like, I don't know, win a million dollars in cash and prizes in the process*. But in the end, I just stammer and stutter. In the end, I've got nothing.

But Trey? Trey's got a lot more to say. "Look, I know none of us want to imagine something bad's happened to them, and that's okay. But also we have to start thinking more about ourselves. We've gotta start worrying more about each other, and what we can all do to support each other. And right now, Sissy, we're all exhausted and in my opinion, the best thing we can do is rest up and try again another time."

Sage wags her head. "Yeah, but *when*?"

"When we're ready," Trey continues. "Whatever's out there," he adds, looking back toward Witch Woods, "we can't face it if we're not ready. We've gotta be at our best."

Sage nods slowly as we all climb back into the car.

No one says a word until we're seconds from pulling into my driveway. "But what if they need us?" Sage asks quietly. And then, as if not naming *why* they might need us left too many awful possibilities to face, she adds, "What if there's been an accident?"

I pull the car back into the driveway and Trey hops out to pull open the garage door.

I turn in my seat and meet Sage's bright brown eyes. "Don't worry," I tell her. "We'll try again soon. I promise. Everything's gonna be okay."

I say this aloud and pause, waiting for someone to interrupt and tell me I'm crazy, that there's no way I can possibly know *everything's gonna be okay*, let alone that *we'll* be okay.

"In the meantime," Sonia finally adds, "there's so much we need to do around our camp."

Everyone climbs out of the car, except for me.

I pull into the garage and turn off the engine. And I just sit there a second, staring at my friends in the rearview mirror, staring out at the long stretch of road behind them.

And it's like I'm waiting for something to happen.

As if, any minute WBD and Mom were gonna breeze down Ellison Ave in Mom's minivan, grinning like they never left, half of WBD's head hanging out the window as he howled off-key to the radio. You know how you're rocking to your favorite song when suddenly your parents are banging on your door, on the wall, on the ceiling like, *Turn that noise down, you're gonna rupture your eardrums with all that racket?* Yeah, that's how I feel about WBD's music.

The only thing WBD spends more time on than over-cleaning his car—singing and dancing.

Which you're thinking, *Well, then that must mean he's really good at singing and dancing, right?*

WRONG! You have never been more wrong about anything in your natural-born life!

Trust me, he is the exact opposite of really good. And even that doesn't do justice to the amount of irreparable harm he's brought to eardrums and eye sockets everywhere.

The man's singing and dancing is a very real threat to national security!

Once, a few months back, me and The Bronster saw a dark car parked in front of our house with a man and woman wearing equally dark suits sitting inside it, and Mom claimed they were door-to-door ministers but I'm pretty sure they were Secret Service agents from the government sent to investigate the global impact of WBD's notoriously awful singing and dancing.

In fact, that's probably why there were two of them. One was from the Department of Dangerous Dad Dancing and the other was from the Office of Vocal Villainy. You're not gonna convince me otherwise.

All that said, the truth is, right now, in this moment as I take one last look at WBD's car before I pull down the garage door—I'd willingly subject myself to that cruel and unusual song-and-dance torture if it meant going back to the good old days where having fun was the only thing I had to worry about.

6300

Somehow, some way, no matter what it takes, we all agree we're getting to the beach.

And yes, partly because we promised Sage so she'd let us leave behind the creepy woods, but alsoooo, we all know that the beach, aka the last place our family, friends, and town supposedly were gathered before they disappeared, is obviously the key to this whole mystery.

So, the very next morning after our foray into Witch Woods, it's decided.

Operation: Get to the Beach is back on!

And by *we all agree*, I mean, 80 percent of us agree. Yep, for those of us who don't dress up as human calculators for Halloween, or if you just prefer fractions like a weirdo—that means that four-fifths of us are in complete agreement, while the remaining one-fifth is kind of an idiot.

I'm joking, I'm joking.

None of us are idiots. That was rude of you to laugh at that. Name calling is never okay. Never! I hope you're ashamed, doo-doo face.

Sorry, I couldn't resist.

~~~

Our first attempt starts well.

We're cruising in WBD's car, feeling fairly optimistic, everything going according to plan. And then bad things happen and it all turns to a heaping pile of crap nuggets.

But let's start from the top.

I'm driving and we're approximately seven minutes down the road when, out of nowhere, the car is swarmed by killer bees. Except when I say swarmed, you're probably imagining the bees are *outside* the car, trying to find a way inside, right?

Nope. Worse. Somehow, the bees are *already in* the car.

It's the only explanation; if they'd come through the windows, we would've noticed.

Instead, I hear *bzzz bzzzz* on the side of my face. I assume it's Xavier being stupid, blowing in my ear or whatever, trying to scare me. "X, quit, bro," I say when the *bzzz* gets louder. That's when I hear *SMAAACCCK* from the other side of the front seat. I glance over and Sonia's palm is now flat against her reddened cheek, yellowjackets attacking her from all sides. I let go of the wheel to swat them away, but the car swerves toward the sidewalk, and I quickly retake control, just in time.

"Are you okay?" I ask Sonia.

I see the fear in Sonia's eyes. "It tried to sting me."

She says *it* meaning she doesn't realize there are many bees. I figure it's probably not the best time to break the news, but also, I've gotta do *something*.

But my brainstorming's interrupted by a louder *SMAAACCCK*. This time it's Sage in the back seat. Then another swat-and-miss, this time it's Trey. And it's at the exact same time as Xavier's heart-piercing scream that I remember one scary fact about my best friend: He's deathly allergic to bees.

I pull the car over as Xavier flips out in the back seat.

"Get them off me! I can't get stung!" He's crying out, jerking his body violently in the exact way I'm pretty sure you're not supposed to when being attacked by killer bees.

"Don't panic, man," Trey is saying. "You're gonna get stung."

Sonia swivels in her seat. "He can't! He's allergic." She points to the blanket the three of them are sitting on. "Quick, put that over you, Xavier."

And in seconds, Xavier's wrapped in a makeshift beekeeper's uniform, most of his skin protected.

Meanwhile, I hop out the car, fling open the rear door, and out dives Trey, Xavier escaping behind him.

"Ohmigod, you okay, bro?" Trey exclaims.

Xavier doesn't answer.

"Where's your EpiPen?" Sonia asks him.

Xavier shakes his head, like he's ashamed; his face looks lighter, probably the fear draining the color from his skin. "I . . . I . . . I forgot it," he admits.

But Sonia wraps him in a hug. We all do, until we're one giant group hug, all of us taking turns promising Xavier *it's okay, you're okay, we're okay.*

"Where did those bees come from?" Sage asks.

I shake my head. "Beats me."

"Maybe there's a hive in the car somewhere," Trey suggests. "We had a bunch of bees bully their way into our house last summer. We had to call the exterminator and crash in a hotel for the weekend."

"Sheesh," I say. "Well, yeah, maybe you and I can search it before we head back?"

Trey nods. "Let's do it."

But Xavier shakes his head. "I'm not getting back in that car until I have my EpiPen."

Sonia squeezes his shoulder, then glances over at me. "How about while you and Trey search the car, the three of us will walk back to the camp?"

We turn over every inch of WBD's ride and find absolutely zero traces of bees.

6400

The next day our second Get to the Beach attempt goes down like our first.

Except this time it starts with a killer wardrobe change.

Wait, what?

Sounds wild, I know. Let me explain.

It all starts with Xavier, who after the bees incident is unsurprisingly less than excited to continue our little expedition. "Ha! You guys are crazy if you think I'm getting back in that death trap," he says firmly, nodding toward WBD's car, his arms folded across his chest.

Which seems fair considering yesterday he almost died.

"Okay, but what if we made you extra protection?" Sage asks.

"Extra protection? How?" Xavier inquires, curious but unconvinced this is even a thing.

Thirty minutes later, whereas we're all still rocking our same outfits, Sage exits her house with a huge grin.

"Ahem," she says, ensuring she has our attention. "Welcome to Ohio Fashion Week. You're in for a real treat because today we're serving up a whole *look*. Or should I say, Xavier's serving, haha. So without further ado, let's start our show."

Trey, Sonia, and I follow Sage's eyes back to the front door, except nothing happens.

Sage turns back to us and laughs like she's not worried, like this is all part of the show. "X probably just wanted to make sure you guys are actually ready first, haha."

"We're ready," Trey confirms.

"Never been readier," I add.

"Right," she says nervously. "Right." She clears her throat. "Let's try this again. And now, without further ado, let's start our shoooooowwww . . ."

But even with the extra announcer flourish, nothing happens.

Xavier's still nowhere to be found.

"Give me one sec," Sage says, forcing a smile. "Just gonna check on our star."

We watch her slip back into the house, and then a few seconds later, we hear Sage and Xavier clearly arguing, although we can't understand what's being said, even though the three of us all press our ears against the screen.

"They must be in the kitchen," Trey explains. "They're too far away."

Except one minute later, Sage is suddenly at the door and we practically fall back, trying to pretend like we weren't just attempting to eavesdrop.

She shakes her head. "Just had to work out a few details. Our model's dealing with what we in the entertainment biz call *stage fright*."

"Is Xavier okay?" Sonia asks.

Sage nods, a portable speaker suddenly in her hands. "Oh, he's more than okay. See for yourself. Without further ado, Ohio Fashion Week presents the star of our show, Xavvvviiiieeerrrrrrr." Sage taps on the speaker and out pumps some bass-heavy electronic dance music.

And then, the front screen door flies open, and out steps the main attraction—Xavier, rocking thick army-green cargo pants, a gray "Save the Sea Turtles" sweatshirt, and a light brown bucket hat covered in what appears to be a fishing net, the net hanging from the brim of the hat down past Xavier's shoulders. Xavier walks down the runway, aka the sidewalk, his face suggesting he's not at all into it, except his walk is clearly saying otherwise. My man is *stepping fierce*, y'all.

"Xavier's sporting the latest in our Explorer Collection. This 'fit is called 'No Bees, Puh-lese,' and is loosely inspired by a bee-keeper's uniform," Sage announces, obviously really proud of her styling. "What do you think?"

"I think I'm gonna die of heat exhaustion," Xavier mumbles, rolling his eyes harder than should be humanly possible.

"But at least you'll be safe from bees," Sage counters, unfazed by Xavier's grumbling. "Well, almost safe. There's one more thing left to complete your 'fit."

Wanna guess what that one thing was?

Um, well, if you guessed duct taping the ends of the shirtsleeves and the bottom of his pants closed so that, according to Sage, nothing could crawl or fly inside his clothing, then *ding ding ding*, congratulations, you are officially The World's Best Guesser.

"Okay, because this tape is definitely *not* making this outfit even hotter," Xavier complains. "I don't think this is necessary."

"Nonsense," Sage insists, while the other three of us try to hold in our laughter. "Better to be hot than dead, amirite? Plus, Eddie can just blast the AC. You'll be fine, ya big baby."

And she's right, because only moments later, we're back in the car. Yep, all five of us.

And turns out, despite his complaints, Xavier's the best prepared for what happens next.

Remember how I said our second Get to the Beach attempt plays out just like our first? Yep, that's exactly what happens. Except this time, swap out the killer bees for fire ants—an especially bizarre phenomenon, considering in all my twelve years living in Ohio, I've seen approximately negative-zero fire ants here, ever.

So, imagine my surprise as a couple dozen sink their chompers deep between my toes, in my elbows, and behind my kneecaps. Apparently, a bathing suit and flip-flops? Yeah, not the best *end of the world* survival wear.

A particularly vicious fire ant tears into my booty meat and I nearly crash the car into a telephone pole, trying to park and leap out at the same time. We spend an hour smearing anti-bacterial lotion on every inch of our bodies, slathering ourselves in anti-itch, until our skin's like sticky chalk. Lowkey, we look like a collection of amateur pottery.

Well, all of us except—yep, you guessed it—the Looks Server himself, Xavier.

~~~~~

This time Sonia and Sage search the car top to bottom—and guess what:

There are no more secret ant colonies than there are beehives.

We postpone dinner to launch our third attempt, this time

arming ourselves with bug spray and fly swatters and hosing each other down with insect repellant. Ay, bring it on, thou murderous mosquitoes; cometh for us, o' ravenous roaches. We're ready for whateverth.

So of course, this time, zero insects crash our party.

Yay, so you made it to the beach?

I didn't say *that*. Because that's when The Singularly Most Awful Smell in the History of Disgusting, Puke-Inducing Scents—a rich, heavy fragrance best described as *angry skunk* meets *an eight-year-old glass of milk left out in the sun*—suddenly fills the car with the speed and sneakiness of a mom fart. Even with all four windows rolled all the way down, we're choking, gasping for air.

We vote to skip dinner. Turns out when the smell of stale fish poop pellets is trapped in your nostrils, you stop being hungry.

6500

It's kinda hard to rally behind Operation: Get to the Beach when everything smells like the brown mystery "juice" sloshing around the bottom of a trash can.

But Sage still won't let it go. "What, you'd rather sit around and hope all the answers come to us?"

Xavier nods. "Honestly, I love that for us."

"I don't get it, Xavy," Sage says. Which, I'm not entirely sure what's weirder—that she's calling him Xavy or that he seems unfazed by it, but whatever, not my biz. "You're as anxious to find your family as the rest of us, so how come you'd rather stay here than go look for them?"

Xavier shrugs. "We've tried four times now. *Four.* And each time something awful has happened."

Sage shakes her head. "Hold on. Awful? A horrible smell, some angry ants, a few bees? Annoying, for sure, but I'm not—"

Xavier cuts in. "I could've died from those *few bees*, so excuse me if I find it all a bit more than annoying."

Sage frowns. "I didn't mean it that way, Xavy. I'm sorry I—"

But Xavier's already stomping away, cutting across my front yard back toward our camp, which is basically a few tents stuffed with sleeping bags and pillows, all surrounding a large campfire where we cook and eat.

"Welp. Guessing he's out," Trey says. "You could've been a little more chill, Sage. He's right, he's the only one whose life was in actual danger. He's got a right to feel different than the rest of us."

Sage's eyes follow Xavier as he tries out a trio of green-and-white lawn chairs, like a regular Xavy-Locks one after another, before circling back to the first chair and plopping himself down extra dramatically. "You know I didn't mean it like that. I can't help that's how he chose to take it."

Sonia clears her throat. "Maybe you didn't mean it that way, but Xavier's probably scared. If that was me, I'd be, too."

"Same," I agree.

"Me three," Trey chimes.

"Ugggghhh," Sage groans. "Okay, fine. I should've been more . . ."

"Understanding," Trey finishes.

"Empathetic," I add.

"Compassionate," Sonia tags on.

Sage shakes her head. "I was gonna say *more chill*, but go off, I guess."

We all laugh a bit. "You're welcome," I say.

"Anytime," Sonia says.

"Hey," Trey says, nudging Sage in her shoulder. "Maybe you should go—"

"Apologize," Sage interjects. "Already on it." She tears through the grass, toward camp, toward the first green-and-white lawn chair.

The three of us watch as Sage's pigtailed head tips up and down as she deliveries her apology, Xavier's head bobbing back in reply, his face falling into a look that says, *Nope, apology definitely not accepted*. "Uh-oh," Trey says. "Doesn't look like it's going well. Maybe I should help?" Trey takes a step but Sonia stops him, says, "Wait. Give it a sec."

Except whatever Sage and Xavier are saying to each other only seems to grow more intense with every word, every gesture.

I turn to Trey. "Okay, man, maybe you better go step—"

But before I can say *in*, Xavier's head falls backward . . . in laughter. Dude howling like he's just heard the funniest joke of his entire life. Sage is cracking up just as hard.

Trey smiles. "Or I can just chill here and let them figure it out."

Xavier extends his hand and Sage meets it with a fist bump.

"Love me a good make-up scene," Sonia says.

"Yeah, it's great," I say. "Except they're both right. We've gotta get to the beach, yeah?"

Sonia and Trey nod.

I point my chin at Xavier. "But what if we're not so lucky next time? Does anyone else feel like something is trying to stop us from getting there? What if it costs us for real, in a way that changes everything?"

"Maybe," Sonia says, massaging the back of her neck. "But can we afford to *not* try?"

Trey cracks his knuckles. "If we give up on the beach, maybe Sage gets frustrated and tries to go solo again, but if we keep trying, maybe Xavier parks himself in that chair forever?"

"So, we have our answer, then," I say with a shrug. Because as far as I'm concerned, the only thing worse than smelling brown trash juice is another trip to Witch Woods.

6600

On the morning of our fifth and hopefully final attempt, it's Trey's turn to play chef—and not gonna lie, I'm fully expecting him to plop a plastic cup of plain vanilla, zero-fat, zero-sugar, zero-taste yogurt in front of us. Figure if we're lucky, maybe our resident super-athletic health nut will let us cheat with banana slices and a dash of granola on top.

But guys, I was capital *W* Wrong Wrong Wrong.

Because instead, Trey lowers a silver platter of awesome deliciousness onto our outdoor dining table—aka a picnic table we dragged over from the Conroes' yard across the street—an impressive tower of thick golden-brown bread stacked in its shiny center.

"Oooooh," the four of us sing at the same time.

Trey smiles, his shoulders squared, his long arms clasped behind his back. He's practically bouncing on his heels. "I present to you French toast on challah bread, courtesy of Leavened

Bakery, with a fresh strawberry compote on top and drizzled with locally sourced honey from the Bauers' beehives."

"Hold up." Sage flashes her big bro a look. "You for real went to Leavened without me?"

"Sorry, kid. I jog past there on my morning runs. This time I figured I should scrounge up whatever wasn't stale. The challah's still a day or two older than I prefer, but turns out it's hard to get freshly baked bread when the baker's missing, so."

I harpoon a piece of toast and a honey-coated strawberry slice and plunk it into my mouth.

And? How is it, Eddie? you ask.

Well, my friends, all I can say is you know how in the cartoons, a character's eyes will inflate like ten times bigger than normal and bug outta their face?

Yeah, that's what happens when I bite down into Trey's breakfast.

I basically have to push my eyes back into their sockets.

Seriously, we haven't been this quiet together since . . . ever.

Except a few bites in, we all come up for air long enough to say: *OMG, Trey nom nom. This is the nom nom nom best nom nom French toast nom we've ever nom nom had nom.*

And it's like, geez, amazing athlete, ridiculously popular, *and* first-rate chef—what *can't* Trey do?

Anyway, we're all stuffing ourselves with bread and veggie omelets (yep, bro made omelets, too! Had cups filled with various omelet toppings and we each chose what we wanted). Honestly, I was a little disappointed at first, seeing how Trey only had veggies and shredded cheese—"No bacon, bro?"—because ugh, veggies in eggs? What's that about? It's like one of those parent tricks, when it's Tuesday and they serve you "tacos" except you realize it's not ground beef inside, it's chopped-up mushrooms—nice try, WBD, but you can take your secret veggies and your oat milk and beat it, my guy.

Also, how come everything *good for you* tastes lowkey horrible?

If you want me to gobble down some asparagus, how 'bout making it taste like pizza?

So, yeah, we're loving breakfast but Xavier's barely said a word, so I'm like, *Okay, he's not gonna come this morning. He's gonna sit this one out.*

But when we're done eating and we all pile into the car, here he is, walking up my driveway, quietly opening the rear car door.

"You sure?" I ask him just before he ducks into the back seat.

He stares me in the eyes. "Last time. If this doesn't work, I'm out."

I tap him on his shoulder. "I'm glad you're here."

We pile into the car, I turn the key, and the engine roars to life.

We're a half mile down the road, windows down, the early morning breeze rolling in, cooling our faces even as the sun shines brilliantly overhead. And we've been down this road before, literally, but I don't know—somehow it feels different. More hopeful maybe. All I know is everyone's in pretty good spirits, considering the whole world's apparently ending and we're possibly the last humans alive, although maybe not for long if insects and garbage smells have anything to say about it.

And then we hear *BLADOWBLADOOMDOOMP*.

"What was that?" Sonia asks.

Xavier slaps his forehead. "Not again."

Trey sighs. "Now what?"

"Guys, it's probably nothing," Sage sings. "Let's be cool until we know, yeah?"

Turns out we have a flat tire, which, okay, not ideal but also not, you know, the end of the world—because, again, that seems to already be happening, so. But yeah, this is clearly random bad luck, right? There's nothing remotely weird about a flat tire, yeah?

That's what we thought, too, at first—

And then Trey's like, "Wait, the rear tire on my side is flat, too."

So's the one on Sonia's side.

Which is when we realize we aren't dealing with *one* flat tire.

Nope, somehow, *all four* tires are completely flat and as far as we can tell completely unrepairable.

Not that we could repair them even if they were.

And I can see it all over Xavier's face. That *I told ya so* expression as bright as a flashing neon sign outside a bowling alley. Meanwhile, Sage's entire body is practically buzzing with frustration.

"We can't just leave WBD's car out here in the middle of the road like this," I say.

"Okay, but we can't push it on four flat tires," Xavier says, adjusting his half-fro from wilting in his eyes.

"We'll change the tires out here," Sonia says, already turning around and walking back toward camp.

"Where are we gonna find four replacement tires?" Sage asks.

And Sonia, without turning around or looking back, simply replies, "The tire shop, obviously."

My eyebrows arch. "You mean, Spinelli's dad's shop?"

Xavier wags his head. "But how are we gonna get inside?"

"Don't worry," Sonia calls back. "I've got a plan."

Which makes me feel better, because in case you missed it, Sonia's kinda the unofficial brains of this operation. If she's got a plan, feel free to kick back and take it easy, your problem's as good as solved.

6700

A crowbar?

This can't be The Plan.

Except Sonia's cheesing so hard, you'd think she just handed me the key to time travel—and you know, not guaranteed tetanus.

Tetanus, Eddie? Sounds like a fun video game.

Yep, it's exactly like a video game, if that video game's a bacterial infection triggering involuntary muscle spasms, fever, and difficulty swallowing.

Okay, how'd you know all that without *the internet?*

Groan. I guess I picked it up from WBD. Did I mention he's a nurse?

Oh, I didn't?

Hey, guys, WBD's a nurse.

And to be honest, the way things are going, it would be great to have a nurse around . . . even if it's my Wanna-Be Dad.

Man, why didn't I hang back with the other guys? I could be taking a "power nap" under a shady tree like Trey. I could be doing whatever everyone else is doing . . . Okay, who cares if I don't even know what they're doing? It's gotta be better than this. Why am I here, holding what has to be one of the most specific, most useless "tools" on the planet when I could be kicking back at camp, sipping iced tea, and going in on X's haircut?

"Soooo . . ." I turn the crowbar over in my hands. "Are we gonna trade this for something useful?"

"Haha, very funny, Eddie."

"Oooh." I wave it like a wand. "Is it a *magic* crowbar?"

"You got it!" Sonia chirps, nodding way too enthusiastically. "It has the power to make you stop asking stupid questions." She snaps her fingers as if summoning the question-stopping spirit. Honestly, I wish there was an all-powerful, stupid-question-stopping spirit. Can you imagine? We'd never have to suffer through another parent/teacher/random-old-person interrogation again.

"I feel kinda bad breaking in," I say, slapping the metal crowbar in my palm, rust flakes floating down onto my flip-flops like fish food shaken into a tank. "Spinelli's so cool."

Sonia nods. "Spinelli *is* cool, yes. Which is why, under the present circumstances, I think Spinelli and her dad would be cool with us borrowing four tires. But if it makes you feel better, how 'bout you leave a note?"

"Maybe I will." Except my swim trunk side pockets are *empty*. "Um, you got a pen?" I check my lone back pocket. "And paper?"

"Dude," Sonia says, ignoring my questions with a skill that apparently all older siblings must learn—yep, Sonia's got a brother and sister, aka The Terror Twins. Wanna take a stab at how they earned that nickname? As much as I love hanging at Sonia's house, The Terror Twins are so bad, they *almost* make me appreciate The Bronster. I repeat, *almost*.

"Hey, do we even know how to change a tire?"

Sonia sighs. "If by *we* you mean *me*, yes. You know how my mom is."

I laugh because I do know. Sonia's mom's the kind of parent whose favorite sentence is: *Come watch me do this random thing so you know how to do it on the small chance you need it.*

Sonia clears her throat—*"Ahem"*—and waves me toward the shop door, and I thrust the crowbar skyward like a sword only seconds from its first battle. I slide the crowbar into the gap between the door and its frame, and it hangs there, suspended in air, pointing at me like a giant robot finger.

"Anytime you wanna start," Sonia says, behind me.

"You wanna do this?" I say, whirling back to meet her eyes, which she's rolling so hard someone's parent somewhere is muttering, *They're gonna get stuck up there.*

Sonia takes a step forward, holds out her hand. "I'll gladly do it."

But I block her path. "I think Spinelli would want me to do this."

Sonia shakes her head. "What are you talking about?"

I give her a look like, *Please, I need silence, I'm trying to focus,* and Sonia looks like she might snap, but instead she growls and bites her tongue.

I take a deep breath. Waggle my arms to loosen up my shoulders.

You got this, Eddie, I say to myself.

I crack my neck left, then right. Take one more deep breath.

You were made for moments like this, myself says back to me.

I spread my fingers wide and wrap them around the rusty crowbar. "Count me down," I say over my shoulder.

"Um, count me out," Sonia shoots back.

SELF: *All good, Eddie. Ignore the haters. Count yourself down, bruh.*

    Great idea, Self, I say to myself because sometimes I call myself

Self for short. Thanks!

SELF: *Don't mention it. It's what I do.*

*Don't you mean what **we** do?*

SELF: *Oh yeaaaaah, now you're talking to me.*

ME: *Can we just do this already?*

SELF: *Sorry, our bad.*

"Three . . ." I say, initiating the countdown.

I grip the crowbar more firmly.

"Two . . ."

I loosen my fingers, then retighten.

"One . . ."

I jerk the crowbar toward my chest, real confidently—the way a treasure hunter pulls a hidden lever—and *BLOOP!* I pop open the door, like a boss. I flip the crowbar down the sidewalk several feet away, like a batter who's just obliterated a fastball like it's nothing, like blasting baseballs into outer space is the same as breathing to me; I do it in my sleep.

"Are you done?" Sonia says, folding her arms across her chest, trying her best not to smile because sometimes she's a hater like that.

"Am I done?" I repeat. "I'm just getting started, baby," I say, now pumping my fist at the crowd in celebration as I round the "bases," prancing around the shop parking lot, before squeezing between the two golf carts we borrowed from Sonia's neighbor—is there anything more fun than whipping a golf cart around?! No, the answer is NO!—and frog-leaping onto "home base," back where I began. "*Now* I'm done." I hold up a high five to Sonia.

"Eddie." She shakes her head like she can't believe what she just saw. "Why you so dumb?" But this time she can't help but laugh, slapping her hand against mine, because sometimes she's a friend like that.

Anyway, I know I made it look easy buuut there are a couple more steps I left out. Don't worry, I've helpfully listed them out for you, should you ever encounter the end of the world and need to force entry into a building. Otherwise, keep in mind, this is highly illegal.

- **Step 1:** Wedge a crowbar into the doorframe.

- **Step 2:** Pull crowbar *really, really* hard.

- **Step 3:** Lift weights.

- **Step 4:** Grow muscles. Specifically, biceps.

- **Step 5:** Flex in the mirror and smile and ask your reflection: "You get your tickets yet?" Your reflection says, "Tickets for what?" And you, flexing hard enough to burst a blood vessel, reply: "For the gun show!"

- **Step 6:** Repeat step 2.

- **Step** 7: Door splinters open.

- **Step 8:** Take a bow.

- **Step 9:** Kiss your biceps. Yep, *both*.

The inside of the shop is a tire lover's paradise. Rows of tires line every wall! Monster truck tires! Tires stacked eight feet tall like towers of rubber donuts! Leaning towers, too, like they're italicized! Skinny tires! Bike tires! Tires hanging from the ceiling! Tractor tires! A bucket of lawn mower tires! There are more tires here than there are cars in Carterville!

Uhh, Eddie, probably because you need four tires for every car, right? Making that a 4:1 ratio, yeah?

Obviously, I know that. I was only being—you know what, hold, please. O' Great and Powerful Stupid-Question-Crushing Spirit, I, Eddie Gordon Holloway, now call upon you . . .

~~~

Two tires bungee-corded to each golf cart, Sonia climbs behind the wheel and I'm about to slide into mine when I suddenly remember. I hurry back through the shop door.

"What's wrong? Where ya going?" Sonia yells after me.

A moment later, I'm taping a piece of paper to the shop window right next to a sloppily written *BE BACK AFTER BEACH BASH* sign.

Maybe Sonia was only joking earlier, but I wasn't. I do feel kinda bad. Maybe it's corny, but I still wanna do right by my family and friends—even if they aren't here right now.

> We O.U. 4 car tires! Thanks!
> Sincerely,
> Eddie and friends
> p.s. Oh, plus, a new door lock! Sorry!

When we finally pull up to camp in our golf carts, the last thing I wanna do is work.

"What a day," I say, grabbing my Real Dad's toolbox off my cart.

"What a day," everyone mutters as we roll up our sleeves and get to work.

"But you know what they say about tomorrow," Xavier says as he pumps the hydraulic jack arm, lifting the back right side of the car off the pavement.

"What's that?" I ask.

"It's always a new day," Xavier says, a small smile appearing on his face.

And yeah, maybe under normal circumstances we'd give each other crap for being so corny, but honestly, I think we all know we need all the good vibes we can find, cheesy or not.

Xavier and I bump fists. "Facts," I agree.

Facts.

6800

As we sit around the campfire roasting marshmallows and chowing down on s'mores, I can't help but think how weird it is that only nine hours ago, we *needed* to get to the beach.

We were *desperate* for the beach.

We had questions and we couldn't get there fast enough for the answers.

Where is everyone?

When are they coming back?

Why didn't they take us with them?

Honestly, we'd have settled for *an* answer.

Even a hint would've been something.

Of course, there's the possibility we get to the beach and find nothing.

No people. No pets. No clues.

But c'mon, guys, what are the odds of *that*? Five percent? At worst, 10? The chances of *absolutely nothing* are laughable, right? I mean, yeah, right. Nothing?! Hahaha!

I'm no math whiz, but the chances are slim, yeah?

Except suddenly it's like the five of us couldn't be more deflated.

In half a day, we'd gone from being the world's largest inflated balloon to a sad, collapsed rubber blob, not knowing we had a hole in us from the very beginning.

That this whole time we've been leaking air and losing hope.

"Is it weird that I kinda just wanna stay home now?" Trey asks.

"No," I say, knowing that deep down I feel the same way. "It's not weird at all."

"Maybe we hold off on the beach," Sonia adds.

Sage shakes her head. "No, we can't give up! We can't quit!"

Sonia swivels in her seat to face Sage. "Just until we figure out a little more."

"But how are we gonna figure anything out by staying home?" Sage demands, folding her arms.

"You ever wonder maybe the reason we haven't made it to the beach yet is because we're not supposed to?" Xavier wonders aloud. "That something's intentionally stopping us?"

Normally, we'd all chime in with a theory, share whatever it is we're thinking, but nope, no one says a word. Instead, we sit in silence, our bodies pointed away from each other in nearly every direction, like a human compass.

6900

All I'm saying is, clearly, we're in a bad spot.

We're all alone with zero clue where everyone else is.

You ask me, we've got two choices.

Suck on these ultra-sour lemons life's thrown at us—or toss those bad boys into a juicer, add sugar, and sip on some oh-so-refreshing, perfectly sweet lemonade.

Translation, Eddie?

Either we make the most of a bad situation and try to enjoy ourselves as much as humanly possible—or we lie down and feel sorry for ourselves and slowly slip into the cold, cruel pit of super sadness . . .

The decision's pretty easy, if you ask me.

So, this is my mission: keep everyone out of their feelings, out of the pit, and outta-this-world happy.

7000

Now you're probably wondering, Eddie, what does everyone do when the vibes are off? How do y'all pass the time? Or maybe even more importantly . . . *where* do y'all pass the time?

Well, you're all the way in luck, because not only can I answer your question, I can also lighten the mood at the same time. That's right, my friends, it's time we treated y'all to a tour!

Hi, guys, I'm your host, E-Geezy—and this is *Super Survivor Swag Pads*, the show where we give you never-before-seen access to some of the coolest places on the planet to hole up while the world ends all around you. Trust me, you're not gonna wanna miss this.

First off, as y'all know, I've got four roommates. Sure, there's enough space for everyone to have their own spot, but so far we're sticking together, camp-style. So, first up, Xavier's X-Tra Spicy but Also Relaxing Wonderland Oasis.

Now to some, this might look like just a whole lotta green grass two or three days from needing a visit from Mr. Lawn Mower, but for my boy X, this grassy slice of backyard is a meditation paradise. But you don't have to take my word for it. Here's X himself. What up, X?!

X: *Hey.*

E-GEEZY: *Tell us about your crib, bro.*

X *looks left, then right*: *It's grass.*

E-GEEZY *smiles nervously into the camera*: *Right, right, but tell the people what makes this section of grass X-tra Special.*

X: *I've got three lawn chairs that look the same but sit different. Lemme show you . . .*

E-GEEZY *starting to walk away*: *Okay, well, that was awesome. Thanks, X. Next up is—*

X *popping back in front of the camera*: *This chair sits kinda hard, so if you like firm support, you might enjoy this one. This second chair is a bit saggy, so if you're into . . .*

E-GEEZY: *Thanks again, X. Love those chairs. Now next up is—*

X *swivels the camera back onto his face*: *My personal favorite chair's the middle one because it's not too firm or too soft. It's just right. Also, this grass, I'm pretty sure it's Kentucky bluegrass, which is incredibly gentle on the skin. It's like sleeping in a bed of lotion.*

E-GEEZY *laughs nervously as he resumes walking away*: *Moisturizing while you sleep, amazing. Next up: Sage's Sanctuary.*

[The camera follows Eddie to the backyard, where a large red tent flutters in the breeze. A handwritten sign that says *Beach Brainstorming in Progress* is duct-taped to the door flap.]

E-GEEZY: *Knock, knock, anybody home?*

SAGE *from inside the tent*: *Enter at your own risk!*

[We follow E-Geezy and enter the tent. Inside, the walls are covered in crayon, marker, and colored-pencil drawings of ways to get to the beach. There are also several maps of Carterville with gold star stickers stuck to locations. Sage is sitting on an upside-down laundry basket at her "desk"—a wooden TV tray, where she's scribbling a new plan.]

E-GEEZY: *So this is where the beach plotting happens. How's it going, Sage?*

SAGE: *Well, we haven't made it to the beach yet, despite my best efforts, so you tell me.*

E-GEEZY: *Okay, well, thanks for the quick peek. Good luck! Next up: Trey's Tower of Power.*

[The camera follows E-Geezy as he walks over to another tent, this one built atop two picnic tables that have been pushed together.]

[Trey grunts as he power-lifts a large semitruck tire over his head.]

E-GEEZY: *So, Trey, the people wanna know, why set up your tent on tables?*

[Trey drops the tire with a thud.]

TREY: *Two reasons, my man. One, keeps you safe from predators. Two, at night, when I'm lying down, I like to be as close to the stars as I can be, you know? Thinking of building a tree house, too. Now if you'll excuse me . . .*

[Trey picks up a jump rope and begins hopping in place.]

E-GEEZY: *Oh wow, you just heard a* Super Survivor Swag Pads *exclusssivvveee. Might our next episode feature Trey's Tree House of Triumph? Stay tuned. But before we go out on a limb, haha, we've got your first look at . . .*

[E-Geezy walks past an extinguished firepit to an army-green tent. He unzips the front flap and invites the camera in.]

E-GEEZY: *Welcome to Eddie's Enclave of Exes. That's right, this place is ex-traordinary, ex-ceptional, and ex-ceedingly ex-tra.*

[Inside Eddie's tent, there's a fuzzy blue rug, an unmade cot stacked with more decorative pillows than your mom's bedroom set, a movie projector aimed at a white sheet hanging on the wall, and a mini cooler-fridge. E-Geezy taps on the freezer door and it pops open like magic.]

E-GEEZY: *Sparkling water?*

[E-Geezy flops onto his cot, sending pillows flying everywhere, tucks his hands beneath his head, and sighs.]

E-GEEZY: *There's no place like home, you know? But wait a minute, there's more!*

[Camera follows E-Geezy across his front yard, down a couple houses to Sonia's Garage/Driveway. We see rows and rows of super-organized, super-stacked goods. There are battery-operated fans, gardening tools, and even a row of real astronaut snacks.]

E-GEEZY: *As you can see, Sonia's got your end-of-the-world survival kit covered. Show us around, Sonia.*

SONIA *nodding at a golf cart with a caravan of wagons tied to the back of it*: *I'm really busy. Just got a load of microfleece blankets, first aid kits, and frozen tacos.*

E-GEEZY: *Can never have enough tacos, haha.*

SONIA: *Wait, you think we need more?! I knew I should've packed another wagon's worth. I'll go back to the store this afternoon and . . .*

E-GEEZY: *Well, friends, this has been a special edition of* **Super Survivor Swag Pads: End-of-the-World Camp Style.** *Thanks for tuning in and as always,* **Don't just survive, thriiiiive.**

7100

Well, that tour was about as exciting as a double-mashed-potato sandwich with extra mash on the side.

Yikes, Eddie. You okay, man? Because that was just rude.

You're right and I'm sorry, guys, I don't mean to be a hater, I really don't, but ...

Hmmm, how can I explain my current state of non-well-being?

Woop, I got it. Okay, so you know how hungry people get hangry? Well, I get *hongry*.

Umm, hongry?

Hongry is when you're so hot, you just get angrier and angrier.

And right now, this midafternoon, it's so hot, my fingernails are sweating.

Seriously, do you have any idea how hot it has to be for your fingernails to sweat?!

Honestly, me either, I always get Celsius and Fahrenheit mixed up, but trust me, I wouldn't wish this kind of heat on my worst enemy. Wait, that's a lie, there's a high probability I'd wish it on The Bronster; okay, whatever, so I wouldn't wish this heat wave on my *second* worst enemy.

True story, last week, on a hotter-than-necessary afternoon much like today, I was trying to cut the grass as quickly as possible because (1) grass-cutting sucks; I get it looks cool, but unless you're flexing in a tricked-out riding mower, cutting the grass basically only exists for stores to sell us allergy pills, which sounds crazy I know, but trust me, I read all about it in someone's IG story, and (2) I was trying to get back to the more important business of playing a little game called *Dragon Insurgents II*, so yeah, I was lit-ter-rah-lee darting across our yard whipping our ancient-basically-down-to-three-good-wheels lawn mower up and down and creating what can be safely called The Most Ludicrously Lopsided, Criminally Crooked Rows in the History of Horticulture (which no, horticulture is *not* the study of a dope underground indie music scene that some cool kids dubbed *horti*. Sadly, I'm 97.3 percent positive it's just a dumb fancy word for plant life) . . .

Whatever. The point is: I was so *HOT*, guys . . . Ahem, I said, I was so *HOT*, guys . . . Hello, you're supposed to reply, *How HOT were you, Eddie?* and then I say something kinda witty and hopefully charming. Got it?

So, yeah, I was so *HOT*, guys!

Are we really doing this? We have to. We know he'll never move on otherwise, so. Okay, fine. How hot were you, Eddie?

I was so hot you could've baked cookies in me. Man, I was so *HOT* . . . Man, I was so *HOT* . . .

What, again?! OMG, this guy . . . Sigh . . . How hot were you?

I was so hot, for a second I thought I'd somehow teleported aboard a highly experimental rocket ship right before it foolishly blasted through a field of cosmic rays (shout-out to all my fellow Human Torch fans, iykyk).

Yo, but seriously, I was so *HOT* . . .

How hot?

Not the right line or volume, but all good, we'll let it slide. I was so *HOT* I was sweatier than a cat trying to bury his poop in a tiled floor.

Okay, I stole that last one from Mom. Shocking, right? You'd never expect that from my mother, seeing as her sense of humor is, how do you say, she doesn't have one?

But man, when she hits, she *hits*.

And I can't believe I'm saying this but honestly, right now, I'd be cool with Mom rattling off a million awful, super not jokes back-to-back-to-back if it meant she was here. If it meant she could be home with me, where she belongs.

Oh, Eddie, we're so sorry . . .

Huh? What? Oh, yeah, no, it's cool, guys. *I'm* sorry for bringing the mood down. The whole reason I was saying all that in the first place is because on one of the hottest days this summer, where am I, your boy Eddie Gordon Holloway, currently standing?

Smack-dab in front of a raging, blazing, fireball-roaring, flame-shooting inferno.

7200

I bravely dump a bag of frozen chicken nuggs onto the red-hot grill.

I slice and dice potatoes into thin shoestring fries.

See, it's my turn to cook and what better way to boost the mood than a few crowd-favorite dishes, even if it means standing over *burn-your-eyebrows-off* flames?

I even throw on semi-fresh veggies from the veggie stand two blocks over because as much as I can get down on nuggs and fries any day, all day—squash, peppers, and zucchini probably have a better shot at keeping our bodies and brains sharp.

I even manage to grill-bake a very lopsided chocolate cake complete with thick fudge frosting, chocolate chips, and sprinkles.

This is a meal that would normally spark a standing ovation, but today, right now, man, it barely scores four forced half smiles, and even those are hard to notice considering everyone's making it a point to *not* look at me. It's like they're playing a game called No, No, That Ain't It.

"So, you guys *aren't* in the mood for nuggs and taters?" I ask, adding a bigger-than-necessary grin, so now, between the five of us, we have three whole awkward smiles.

(Yikes, not me doing math during summer vacation.)

Trey rocks nervously on his heels, then says, "Sorry, bro, this looks great, but . . . I think I'm gonna skip dinner and hit the bed for the night. I'll help you clean up first."

"No, no," I say, keeping my smile alive, barely. "I get it. You're tired. We're all tired. It's no big deal. It's just basic stuff, anyway. You should get some rest."

He nods, pats my shoulder, and slinks off to his sleeping bag. Sage, saying good night, trails after her brother.

"Wow, it looks sooo good, bro," Xavier says.

I smile. "Well, dig in, before it gets cold."

X frowns. "But uh, I'm gonna pass, too. I'm crazy wiped."

Except he must notice my face dropping because he quickly adds, "Know what, actually I'd love a few fries first . . ."

"Xavier, it's okay," I assure him. "Today was a lot. You won't hurt my feelings if you wanna go to bed."

"You sure?"

I nod. "Rest up, bro." I throw him a fist bump. "See you in the morning."

I watch him walk away toward his tent, on the other side of the campfire. I pop a nugget into my mouth, and honestly, it's pretty decent, considering my only other "cooking" experience is tossing pizza rolls into our family air fryer. Just last Friday, I made a huge pile of those bad boys for me and Mom—of course she *had to* invite WBD to join us, even though I had definitely *not* accounted for *three* people eating, which meant *considerably less* rolls for me, but okay, Mom, go off, ask the whole neighborhood over for dinner while you're at it—

The whole neighborhood, ha. Can you imagine?

Man, I'd give up pizza rolls forever if it meant everyone suddenly showing up.

So we're clear, I'm talking about sacrificing *supreme* pizza rolls—green peppers are *naaasssty* and cooked onions should be illegal contraband, punishable by some form of public humiliation—

Not those perfectly proportioned pepperoni pizza rolls. I'm nostalgic, not crazy.

I'd forgotten I wasn't alone until Sonia says my name.

I snap out of it in time to see her shove a handful of fries into her mouth. "These fries are really good," she says, except it sounds more like *theiszzz fwieszzz arrrgh wheelie gud.*

"You don't have to do that," I say softly, even though I want her to, even though her doing it is making me happy in a way I didn't know I needed until right now.

She pauses her chomping to give me a funny look. "Do what?"

I shrug, my cheeks heating up, because now I feel weird that I said anything. "You know, eat just 'cause everyone else bailed."

"Um, you're kidding, right?" She glances back at our tents, before returning her eyes to me. "You know I'd never pass up an opportunity to . . . stuff my face . . . with fries."

We both laugh and over Sonia's shoulder I watch the moon slip a patch of purple clouds and now it's a spotlight beaming on us. She tilts her head at me, her face in deep concentration like a doctor sliding their stethoscope around your back, listening to you breathe.

"You okay?" I ask her, because yeah, I wanna know, but also to break the weirdly awkward silence—weird because nothing's ever awkward with us, silence included.

She waits a beat before slowly nodding her head. "You?" she says back, softly.

My eyes drift left and right, taking in the (now empty) houses around the cul-de-sac. It's hard to believe how much, how quickly, our literal whole world's changed.

"Yeah," I hear myself answer. "I think so."

She dunks a nugget into a pool of honey mustard, half of which ends up *outside* her mouth, an impressive mustard blobbing her top lip, and I laugh.

"What?" she asks, her face twisting in embarrassment. Another thing that never happens between us—we're never embarrassed around each other, not even when ridiculously embarrassing things happen to one of us.

"Nothing," I say, unable to stop giggling.

"You're giggling," she says, shaking her head. "Better be careful, giggling's one baby step away from snorting."

Instinctively, I lift my hand toward her face, toward her upper lip, and then catch myself—because um, can you say *personal space*, Eddie? Instead, I point to my own upper lip and say, "You've got some sauce there. A mustard mustache."

Only she doesn't wipe it away. "How do you know I didn't do that on purpose?" she asks. "How do you know I don't want a mustard mustache?"

I shrug. "I mean, you've looked worse, so."

She punches me in the arm. "Heyyyy."

My cheeks widen. "I'm teasing."

"Mmhmm," she says as a gust of wind swoops down into our camp.

The wind almost howling, swirling all around us, bringing every non-moving thing to life, fluttering the crinkled edges of aluminum foil the nuggets are resting on, rippling the sides of the nylon tent, making the fingers of the fire sway and dance. We stand there, in the quiet, absorbing everything, taking it all in. This new stillness that's settled atop our neighborhood. Normally, on a beautiful summer night like this you'd hear all kinds of stuff: cicadas strumming, trees rustling, kids bouncing on a trampoline across the street, dogs barking, music floating outta opened windows, the neighbors four houses down watching a movie on one of those inflatable jumbo screens in their backyard.

"So," Sonia says finally, without looking at me. "Do you think we'll ever see them again?"

I nearly ask, *See who?* even though, of course, I know exactly who she means.

"I hope so," I answer. "But the more all this crazy stuff keeps happening, I don't know, the less it seems . . ." I let my voice trail off, afraid to finish the thought out loud.

Sonia passes me a nugget and we chicken-nugget toast each

other. "Cheers," she says, her teeth tearing into the crispy outside.

"Cheers," I repeat, inhaling the nugget in one bite.

"I just keep thinking, we've gotta make our families proud, you know? We've gotta do whatever it takes to survive," she says, still chomping. Sonia, the kind of kid who chews every piece of food 187 times to minimize choking risks and maximize digestion.

Meanwhile, I'm wondering how much chicken's stuck in my teeth. "I don't disagree," I say, trying to free a snagged nugget bit with my tongue, and then going in with my fingers because, man, that chicken's wedged in there tighter than The Bronster's big head in a hoodie. "Whatever it takes."

7300

The next morning, I'm the last to crawl out of my tent.

Everyone else is noshing on breakfast already.

"What are you guys eating?" I ask, de-crusting my eyes.

They all hold up a familiar food and I laugh. "Our boy made some great nuggs last night," Xavier says.

"Don't worry, we saved you some," Sage adds. "And we made tots!"

"Turns out, reheated fries? Yeah, not great," Xavier says.

I slide onto the bench beside Sage. "This is perfect," I say, tossing a nugg into my mouth. "And what are we talking about this junk-food-eating morning?"

"Since when are chicken and potatoes junk food?" Trey asks with a wink.

And I can't help but smile as I chomp on a handful of tots because if athlete and resident health expert Trey is good with this break-fast, who am I to say otherwise?

"We weren't really discussing anything," Trey says. "Sage was showing us her latest Get to the Beach design."

"Yeah, and trying to change everyone's minds about giving it a rest for now," Xavier adds.

"May I?" I say, motioning toward Sage's color-penciled sketch.

"You may," Sage says, handing me the paper.

I'm not sure I completely understand it. There are a lot of moving parts to Sage's plan. But from what I can tell, at one point it involves driving a speedboat eighty miles per hour.

Sonia shakes her head. "Personally, I feel like we're going about this thing the wrong way because we're not thinking about our real problem."

"Which is?" I ask.

Sonia casually tosses a pair of ketchup'ed tots into her mouth, then makes us wait until she's done chewing before continuing her thought. "We're focused on *how* to get to the beach. But isn't the real question, *what's* stopping us from getting to the beach?"

"Wait, what? I'm pretty sure I already said this," Xavier tries to interject, but Sonia keeps going.

Sonia shrugs. "Doesn't it seem weird that no matter what we've tried, we can't seem to even sniff the beach? What if that's because *something* is stopping us?"

Xavier's face twists in annoyance. "Okay, so yeah you definitely stole that theory from me, but it's cool, I don't need credit . . ." And listen, of course, this kinda scary thought crossed all our minds. But does that mean it's something we wanna actually discuss? Like out loud?

No one else is speaking, and in fact, everyone is avoiding eye contact with each other. Welp, guess I have to be the voice of reason here. My hand shoots up in the air. "Um, I vote we change the subject to something less creepy."

"I second that vote," Trey chimes.

Except again, no one is speaking, so again, looks like I'm up to bat.

"Um, well, can you believe this weather we're having? Boy, has it been hot . . ."

Trey clears his throat. "Daily diaries," he says.

"Daily diaries?" I repeat.

Trey nods. "I keep thinking that once this is all over and things go back to normal, we're gonna wanna look back on this whole thing and really meditate on our experience, you know?"

Xavier cackles. "Meditate? Dude, we're twelve."

"And nine," sings Sage.

"Plus, how am I supposed to meditate? I don't even know yoga," Xavier says, wagging his head as if he just made The Best Point Ever Made About Anything.

Meanwhile, the other four of us trade looks like, *Umm, which one of us wants to take this one?* and three sets of eyes lock on Sonia, who sighs because of course we choose her.

"Um, Xavier, you do know meditation and yoga aren't necessarily the same thing, yeah?"

Xavier's forehead wrinkles and his face squeezes together in that way you look when someone has just said something really stupid, and in fact, the thing is so stupid you can't even form words on your tongue strong enough to describe how stupid while also suddenly asking yourself, *Is stupidity contagious?*

I frown. Not because I'm anti-diary writing. I'm not. Dr. Liz, who helps me understand my ADHD, is forever encouraging me to write down my thoughts and feelings as a healthy way to download and safely process them. Is this something I do? Sometimes. Off and on. Usually when my thoughts and feelings are really wild, or are, for whatever reason, difficult to pin down.

"So you're suggesting that every day each of us writes down how we're feeling and what we're going through so that when this weird thing is finally over, we can one day read what we wrote and gain some new understanding about who we were back then, which might lead to a clearer understanding about who we've become?"

"Wow, that was very specific," Trey says, nodding. "But yes, basically. Except who handwrites stuff anymore? Boring and gross."

"Okay, so if we're not gonna handwrite our diary entries, then how exactly do you see this working, Trey?" I ask.

Trey smiles. "We set up another tent and in that tent we set up a camcorder on a stand and collect a few battery packs and at least once a day we all spend a few minutes recording our thoughts and feelings on camera."

"Ohhhhhh, now I get it," I say. "And then one day when all this stuff is finally over, we can all watch what we recorded and gain some new understanding about who we were back then, which might lead to a clearer understanding about who we've become?"

Trey laughs. "Sure, man, yeah. But I was just thinking it would be fun." Trey shrugs. "But also, it could be like therapy, too. Help us deal with everything, instead of keeping it bottled up inside."

Sonia nods. "I love that idea, Trey. But we should also remember that if we need anyone to talk to, we can talk to each other. None of us have to do this thing alone, yeah?"

"Cool," Trey says. "I'll set up the tent."

And so, just like that, it's decided. We'll each record every day for a few minutes. At least until our family and friends and neighbors come back home. Which is either any day now, or you know, never.

And that, my friends, is how the *Carterville Keep It Reels* become a thing.

7400

SAGE'S KEEP IT REEL

At first, I was super bummed I wasn't at Beach Bash when everyone disappeared because:

1. I didn't know if I wanted to be stuck with my annoying brother.
2. I missed my mom and dad.

But then I remembered that nosy Suzy Madison disappeared, too, and I felt a little better.

7500

Operation: Get to the Beach is still paused for now, so after our dinner-for-breakfast we vote to explore Carterville, see what we find.

I'm surprised Xavier's tagging along, but then he says, "What if there are other people out there? What if they need our help?" And I remember that before all this madness, say what you want about X, he's always been a *look out for people* person. I know this from experience; how many times has he had my back, made sure I was good?

Sonia grabs her clipboard, always eager to add more supplies to her already impressive stockpile, because "you can never be *over*-prepared."

Trey's down to ride, so long as he can run alongside the car for the first three miles. "Can't skip cardio, guys," he says, stretching, bouncing on his heels. Seriously, where does this guy get all this energy? This early in the morning? In this July heat? Personally, I don't even wanna run a bath.

Sage caves, despite her protests that "we can't wait too long to get to the beach because what if the clues disappear?"

And me? Well, instead of stressing about getting to the land of hot sand, I have my mission to think of, and that means I just wanna ride around with my friends.

And so the five of us, once more, pile back into WBD's car.

Side note: Breakfast-for-dinner is a classic—everyone loves it and rightly so. But don't sleep on dinner-for-breakfast. I mean, nuggs and tots first thing in the morning? Um, it kinda slaps.

7600

XAVIER'S KEEP IT REEL

Speaking of food slapping, y'all remember how everyone was complaining about that awful smell in the car? The one everyone said made them wanna puke their brains out?

I kinda liked it. If that scent was a body spray, I'd walk around all day sniffing myself.

Honestly, it reminded me of Mom's magic meatless meat loaf. If I could've eaten it, I would've. The smell, I mean, not the meat loaf. Although, obviously, I'd happily devour that, too.

Aw man, now I want loaf.

I'd settle for body spray.

7700

Carterville's a ghost town.

It's legit creepy, driving everywhere, not seeing a single person.

Another strange thing—no electricity means no working traffic lights. Even still, I stop at each one, waiting ten seconds or so, because safety first, amirite?!

That doesn't sound like you, Eddie.

I know. And I was embarrassed to say it the moment it left my lips. Forgive me, please.

Xavier, on the other hand? Not as courteous. "Bro, *who* are you stopping for?" he asks, for the third time in three minutes, which for all my math peeps out there boils down to a one-annoying-question-asked-every-sixty-seconds average.

I nearly say *safety first* again but I catch myself and, instead of rolling to a complete, four-tire stop, I merely slow down to ten miles per hour before zipping through each intersection.

I gotta say, it's way faster, having zero traffic. I highly recommend it.

Driving around, it all *looks* the same: There's the bakery where Trey got the challah bread, there's the tire shop, and Carterville Middle School—always quiet in the summer, except normally there are kids playing baseball on the playground or shooting hoops on the blacktop court, but now it's abandoned, the grass a day or two past needing a cut. We pass by Bullseye, the giant department store where you can buy bedsheets, office supplies, and cantaloupe, all in one trip! No, I'm not extra jazzed about the store, that's just what they say in their commercials. Anyway, Sonia makes us promise to stop there on the way home, because *supplies*, duh. There's the Haunted House Drive-Thru Car Wash (don't ask), the fast-food taco joint, which usually has a long line no matter what time of day, now empty, having closed for Beach Bash.

We're cruising down Oliver Ave when a sudden knock on the car roof nearly separates me from my flip-flops.

I roll down the window. I forgot Trey was jogging. He gives me a look like, *Um, you good, bro?* then points down the road. "Hey, what about the Frankenstein? We should check it out."

I nod. "Good idea. If there's gonna be any house where someone else got left behind, it's gotta be the Frankenstein."

"Race you there," Trey says, already taking off.

I roll up the window and punch the gas.

7800

No, Frankenstein House isn't a secret monster-making laboratory.

Nope, it's not even a *not*-secret monster lab, either—although the owners of the house, Mr. and Mrs. Sutton, are both scientists, soooooo.

But no, it's called the Frankenstein because every time the Suttons have another kid—so far there are eleven of them—they add another addition onto their house, except the additions don't match, so there's red brick, then beige brick, then suddenly white siding, and after that light wood shingles.

So, it's like the house is the monster, get it?

Anyway, the cool thing about the Frankenstein is it basically never sleeps. With that many kids, ages newborn to nineteen, there is always, always action popping off there.

And Mr. and Mrs. Sutton are the kind of parents who want their kids' friends to hang out there, *everyone's welcome here*, so if you're looking for company or you're just bored out of your skull, the Frankenstein's the place to be.

I hop out the car and wink at Trey. "Sorry I had to blow by you like that."

Trey laughs. "Bro, you barely beat me. Race me *before* my morning run, see who comes out on top then."

The other thing about the Frankenstein is the yard is filled with water guns, bikes, scooters, skates, basketballs, baseball bats, on and on and on. They never bother putting anything away because a few seconds later another Sutton kid would just be pulling it back out, which is normally cool because *no cleanup*, but pretty annoying when you're trying to make your way to the porch and nearly lose your flip-flop stepping on a skateboard.

Their yard is a twisted ankle waiting to happen.

We search the front and side yards, and there's nothing.

Trey boosts me to see over the backyard fence and it's empty, too.

We mash the doorbell, but it must be electric because no chime.

"Should we break inside?" Sage asks.

"Umm," I say.

Look, I know I shouldn't feel bad breaking into people's houses; we're doing what we gotta to survive. But I can't help it. I still feel bad.

"Wait, isn't the patio door usually unlocked?" Xavier chimes.

Two minutes later, Trey's boosting me again, but this time it's up, up, annnnnd over. I land with a thud on my butt, losing a flip-flop on my way down. The backyard is less littered than the rest of the yard but only because most of the space is taken up by their humongous deck and massive aboveground pool. I guess when you're a family of thirteen and counting, everything's gotta be bigger than life.

I knock on the patio door, then cup my hands to the glass and peer inside, looking for any signs of life. This house has never been this quiet. It's strange how having driven all over town, the fact that *everyone* really is missing is hitting me inside a . . . house. But I don't know, in a way, it's like the Frankenstein stands for the whole town, so many people normally occupying one space now gone bye-bye.

I turn the patio doorknob and the door creaks open. "Hellooooooo, anyone home?"

The inside of the house, while "cleaner," is just as chaotic as outside. Stacks of books in the black-and-red kitchen, piles of laundry in baskets on the ridiculously long dining room table, a mountain of board games on either side of the two large-screen TVs. That's right, TWO big flat screens, and yes, they watch both at the same time, I've seen it in action. I had a hard time not being distracted by the other TV, but I guess you get used to it when you're constantly competing for space.

I unlock the front door and everyone piles in. We split up the house, opting to go solo rather than partner up. "Otherwise, we'll be looking forever," Sonia says. And we all agree, even though I know she's just in a hurry to get to Bullseye. For a sec, I'm surprised she left her clipboard in the car, but then I see her holding a folded slip of paper, and spot the pen tucked behind her ear, and I realize nope, The Case of the Girl Who Couldn't Get Enough Supplies continues.

I cover my area, the first floor, fairly quickly considering I'd already walked through most of the rooms. But then it hits me.

I hurry back to the dining room and bingo—

Laundry!

If there's gonna be any house with clothes my size, it's gonna be the Frankenstein. At long last, my bathing-suit-wearing days are over. *Hahaha, I can hardly believe my luck*, I think as I pull one of the towering baskets toward me. Why didn't I think of this sooner?

And that's when something else hits me.

And my face twists in horror, my nose twitching in disgust,

because this isn't clean laundry. No, somehow, it's stinkier than my own filthy mound of dirty clothes back home.

Which I would not have thought possible, but here I am, trying to hold back the vomit, gagging with every whiff.

And it occurs to me for the first time, What if I never change my clothes again?!

This *can't* be a thing, me stuck in this bathing suit and flip-flops, okay? How am I supposed to make fun of X's half haircut if I'm suddenly the stinky kid?

We leave the Frankenstein with not much more than we came with. Sonia found their storage room in the basement, but it's mostly dry cereal and canned goods—which according to her master list, we already have plenty of. "Don't worry," she assures us as we back out of the drive, Trey deciding to take a break and join us in the car. "I still completed a full inventory of their supplies, just in case."

And I can't help but think, *No one was worried.*

7900

XAVIER & SONIA'S KEEP IT REEL

XAVIER

Personally, I'm conflicted.

SONIA

Big same.

XAVIER

I mean, on one hand, maybe it's good luck,
Eddie still rocking his bathing suit and flip-
flops after all this time.

SONIA

Right. Maybe it's a superstition thing. Like

when you're on a winning streak and so you do

the same things, eat the same food, style your

hair the same way, wear the same crusty socks

because you don't want to break the streak.

                    XAVIER

          Exactly. Perfect example.

                    SONIA

     But also, it's like . . . I don't know . . .
               it's kind of . . .

                    XAVIER

               Gross.

                    SONIA

     Yes, that. It's definitely giving . . .

                    XAVIER

            Cartoon vibes.

                    SONIA

               Huh?

XAVIER

You know how cartoon characters always wear
the same 'fit, every episode, no matter what?

SONIA

Ohhh, you're right. I was just gonna say
quirky but lovable mascot. But you totes
nailed it with the cartoon vibes.

XAVIER

Sooo, we gonna say something to him
or . . . ?

SONIA

Absolutely not. I'm kinda into it now.

XAVIER

It's kinda like a slow burn. Will our hero
ever change clothes? Won't he? I'm invested.

SONIA and XAVIER fist-bump

8000

I forget about the roundabout until we're there.

What's a roundabout, Eddie?

I'm glad you asked! Basically, it's a circular road where other roads meet.

Huh, we still don't get it, Eddie.

Not to worry, I just so happen to have a handy-dandy diagram I drew up, having anticipated your question. Check it out:

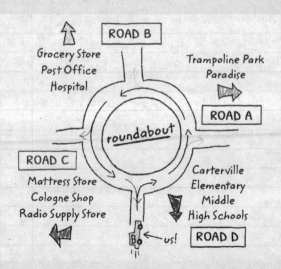

Normally, when the world hasn't vanished, cars constantly loop around, then veer off onto another road.

See, a roundabout is all about choices.

For instance, take the north road and you'll eventually turn up near the grocery store, the post office, and the hospital. Go south (the way we're coming from) and you're close to Carterville's elementary, middle, and high schools. West'll take you to a bunch of boring shops, like a mattress store, a cologne shop that gives me a headache all the way from the parking lot, and a radio supply store that only people over the age of forty-five ever visit.

And to the east, Eddie?

Ah, yes, the east side of our fair town, which just so happens to lead you right to one of my all-time favorite Carterville destinations—

That's right.

Trampoline Park Paradise, home to the bounciest bounce house in all the Mighty Midwest.

"Whoa, so many choices," Sage says. "Which way do we go?"

For *my* money, this is the easiest decision ever.

The right choice is so glaringly obvious you basically need zero brainpower to make it.

It's like asking which toppings you'd rather get on your pizza: pepperoni with extra cheese . . . or a bag of rocks?

It's what The Bronster would call a *no-brainer*.

Which is beyond awesome for my big bro, him somehow stumbling onto something that requires relatively zero real thought and even less consideration, because The Bronster isn't exactly packing a big punch in the brains department, if you catch my drift.

I smile as I prepare to enter the roundabout, meeting Sage's eyes through the rearview mirror. "Well, there's only one direction worth our time . . ."

"Exactly," Sonia agrees. "The radio supply store is the only choice."

I nod. "Right, the radio supply st—" *record scratch*

Hold up, because for a sec it sounded like Sonia suggested skipping Trampoline Park Paradise to fiddle with some stupid radios. So, Sonia likes rocks on her pizza, got it.

Don't get me wrong. Obviously, I really like Sonia. She's one of my best friends. I mean, she's basically family. And now that my blood-related family is gone, she's even more like family. There's not much I wouldn't do for her with zero hesitation. I've got her back, always.

Except right now, Sonia, aka The Person Acting as If We Asked Her to Be Our Leader when, speaking as someone who has been here the *whole time*, we most assuredly did not, is in need of a generous spoonful of the ole medicine I like to call *a reality check*.

Admittedly, I'm not 100 percent sure what's involved in checking someone's grip on reality—but if it's the difference between the radio supply store and Trampoline Park Paradise, hold my oat milk, I'm willing to take a crack at it.

Except before I can object and make my case, Trey drops in his two cents. "I agree. Definitely the radio store. Can you imagine how awesome it would be if we used one of those radios to find some other survivors somewhere?"

Um, no, I cannot imagine this because most people, if they're still out there, aren't wasting their precious time hanging out at a radio supply store, wishing and hoping someone else in another town is doing the same thing at the same time. I'm sorry, but that's just . . . dumb.

And if anyone *is* out there spending their time at a random radio supply store, personally, I'm not sure how excited I am to rush out and meet them, because ugh, can you say *so sad*? Because yuck, can you say *corny*?

Nope, anyone I'd wanna associate with, let alone *hang out and kick it with*, would most assuredly, without question, at this very second, be far too busy nailing a 360, twist-in-midair trampoline super-somersault.

Not that it matters because we're totally gonna miss them, wasting time here, when we could all be getting to know each other over a series of impressively complicated trampoline backflips.

I mean, helloooo, am I missing something? Am I the crazy one here and just don't know it? Seriously, how is this *not* The Easiest Decision Ever Decided in the History of Decision Deciding?

Besides, after all we've been through, the five of us deserve something way better than dusty old radios, amirite or amirite?

"OMG, we're so lucky Eddie brought us this way. I totally forgot about the radio supply store," Xavier says.

"Ha, clearly you also forgot you still need a whole haircut, so I guess you're just a regular ole forgetting machine," I mumble under my breath.

"Huh?" Xavier's face squeezes together in confusion. "You say something, Eddie?"

I shake my head. "Just singing, sorry." Okay, Eddie, how do you redirect these weirdos from a silly radio supply store—honestly, I'm shocked it's still in business—to bounce-house heaven. And then like a lightning bolt, it hits me—the perfect excuse to head east.

"Oh, you know what, guys, we should probably scope out some gas. Trey and I were talking earlier and he knows a way we can siphon gas at the gas station without having power to the electric pumps, so uh, yeah, I'm gonna head east. There's a gas station about a mile or so down the road."

"Wait," Sage says, her eyes squinting in suspicion, "isn't the trampoline park down that way, too?"

I put on my *oh is it, I had no idea* face. "Trampoline park? You're saying there's a trampoline park down here, too? Near the gas station? Well, well, well, I guess it's officially our lucky day, amirite?!"

"Actually, that gas station is the worst," Trey says from the back seat. "My dad said it nearly ruined his car."

"Wait, if we head west, there's a Marigold Gas Station right next to the radio supply store," Xavier offers.

"Perfect," Sonia exclaims, as if Xavier had just solved The Case of the Mysteriously Vanished Town instead of spitting out half-baked directions like an outdated GPS. Because if he knew anything, he'd know there's a car wash *between* Marigold Gas and the radio supply store, ugh. But you know, whatever. Revise the whole map if you want, knock yourself out.

Sonia's face is turned toward her window, but when she looks back, she's almost smiling. "Look, guys, maybe our luck's finally turning. Maybe this is the start of things going our way."

"Yeah, yeah, yeah," I mutter. "I feel *real* lucky."

TO RADIO SUPPLY STORE, OR TO TRAMPOLINE, THAT IS THE QUESTION.

A LIST OF SIMILAR COMPARISONS

- It's like someone seriously asking if you prefer your cereal with or without marshmallows—and you can't even give them a real answer because unfortunately you're way too busy trying not to pass out from laughing too hard. You're laughing so hard, you start coughing—like we're talking serious hacking-up-both-lungs-type coughing.

- It's like someone seriously asking if you prefer showers or baths and you're all, *Umm, bath people are weird. For real, who wants to sit in a tub of dirty water? Like, your dead skin particles are floating in there, and you can see them, gross!*

- It's like someone seriously asking if you'd rather give your school presentation only in front of your class or at a school assembly in front of the entire school, with your family invited!!

Or in other words, do we want to have The Absolute Best Time of Our Young Lives or do we wanna Die of Boredom?

I mean, I'm not trying to put words in anyone's mouth here, but like I said, this feels pretty cut and dried to me. Yep, this is absolutely what you'd call an open-and-shut case. Easy peasy, it's over before it really ever got going. Consider this case all the way closed, my friends.

I mean, how weird is it that the four of them are suddenly so geeked up about finding more supplies, about finding a radio and trying to contact "other survivors" or whatever . . . when just a mile the other way is the real answer to all our problems?

8100

Okay, so you know how in almost every friend group there's always that one super random, ridiculously stubborn friend who just, for reasons entirely unclear, unexplainable, and nonsensical, absolutely REFUSES to get on board with the well-thought-out plan your group just invested invaluable time devising, the plan that everyone else wants to do, and rather than give in and say, *Fine, I'll go along with the plan to keep the peace in the group*, they're all, *I refuse to be any part of this horrible decision and I strongly suggest you guys really stop and rethink what you're actually about to do here because there's a very good chance you're gonna regret it for the rest of your natural-born lives, or at least for a few weeks for sure?*

And you and the rest of the group are doing your best not to explode into an uncontrollable laughing fit because mostly you're good, encouraging, supportive people, but okay yeah, you're also human, too, you never claimed to be perfect, so sure you are also maybe kind of sorta rolling your eyes at each other just a little, it's possible. Like you just said, you're human. You make mistakes, too, okay? Same as anyone. And okay, you are also looking at each other with ginormous smirks plastered onto your faces like, *Oh my goodness, is our friend being for real right now? Gosh, why are they so extra? Seriously, I'd almost forgotten how ridiculously extra they can be, until I was beyond reminded of their degree of extra-ness JUST NOW, and ugh it's a lot, guys, guys, it's soooo much, but also like thank goodness we have each other so we can give each other this look we're giving each other right now and even without a word we can all silently know that we are really incredible humans and incredible friends for even putting up with such a dificult person, we're just saying?*

You know how all that might be a thing that could happen in real life?

Okay, so I thought that was happening just now—

Where I was all, *Okay guys, I think we can all agree the clear choice is to definitely big skip the corny radio supply store and 1,000 percent hit up Trampoline Park Paradise right away, like STAT, which is a word doctors use at hospitals that basically means I NEED YOU TO DO WHAT I JUST SAID, NOT IN A FEW MINUTES, NOT EVEN IN A FEW SECONDS, BUT RIGHT STINKING NOW.*

8200

I'm the last person to walk inside the radio supply store, for obvious reasons.

The first being because I need to sit inside the car and collect myself, because yeah, in case you didn't notice I'm a little frustrated that we're here.

I mean, isn't it obvious that every time we try to do something to solve the *where is everyone* mystery, we just find ourselves in a *bigger* mess?!

Why am I the only one who sees this?!

Anyway, while I've got your attention, I'd love to run a few Get This Radio Store Visit Over with ASAP ideas by y'all while everyone else fiddles with boring, ancient-looking radios.

IDEA #1: Fall on the floor in the middle of the radio store and throw a full-on tantrum, flailing my arms, thrashing my legs hard enough to send both flip-flops sailing, screaming, slapping the tile, grunting, wailing like a fool, you know, the works—until my friends see the light and we go to Trampoline Park Paradise.

IDEA #2: Jump up and down excitedly, like when you really, really need the bathroom before you crap your pants (again), and once they have no choice but to look because *ugh, anything to make this dude quiet down,* you'll say, *Guys, look, look, you're never gonna believe what I just saw across the street. It was our parents, guys. Our parents are back . . . and they're walking to Trampoline Park Paradise because they're probably thinking about where they'd be hanging out at if they had been left behind here, which duh, obviously TPP would be THEE PERFECT "WAIT IT OUT, HOP IT OUT" destination— and okay, I can't be sure but by the way they were walking I'm pretty sure someone told them about the super-secret room with the super bouncy yellow mats, so we should definitely stop gathering supplies like squirrels and get over there STAT!*

IDEA #3: Burn down the radio store.

Ohmigod, stop looking at me like that! Obviously, I'll evacuate the building first.

Um, right, we'd hope so, Eddie. But doesn't that whole deal seem a touch . . . drastic?

Hey, drastic times be like, hello, yes, I'm calling for drastic measures, please.

The saying's desperate *times call for* desperate *measures.*

Drastic. Desperate. Both are thirsty *D* words. Point is, I've gotta do what I gotta—

"AHHHHHHHHHHHHHHHHHH!!!"

Wait, what was that?

Wait, you guys heard that, too? It sounded like a—

Another scream. And then another.

8300

I race down aisle after aisle like my hair's on fire until I nearly crash into Xavier's back.

But it's not just him. Everyone's here, at the back of the store, standing on the customer side of a long bright-blue counter. Their backs are to me, as Trey, Sonia, and Xavier huddle around Sage. Sage, staring at me with a strange, tight smile.

"What's ... what's going on? Who screamed? Is everyone ... Are you guys okay?" I manage to ask, winded from the sprinting and maybe a bit nervous, too.

Sage raises her hand like she's volunteering for something. "Sorry about that. I got a little excited."

I rub my forehead. "I'd hate to see you a lot excited."

"Check this out," Sonia says, holding up a metal-gray box the size of a lunch box, which judging from the speaker grill on the front, I can only assume is a radio.

I'm inches from the counter now. Sonia turns to look at me, and my heart jumps in my chest, because the way her face has hardened, the way her eyes have narrowed, the color nearly drained from her eyes, you would've thought she'd . . .

"You look like you've seen a ghost," I say to her. But Sonia says nothing.

"No, Eddie, we haven't seen a ghost," Trey finally explains. "We *heard* a ghost."

"*Ghosts,*" Xavier clarifies. "We all heard different *ghosts*."

8400

"Okay, will someone please tell me what's going on?"

But no one answers me.

I chew on the inside of my cheek. "Seriously, if you're trying to mess with me, you're doing awesome."

Still not one word, but now they're eyeing each other, like they're taking a silent vote. Finally, Sage sets the radio on the counter, presses a button, and it hums to life.

As Sage turns a small dial and static crackles from the speaker grill, I play a solo round of Guess What Everyone's Excited About. "Let me guess, you guys found a working radio station, right?"

Trey shakes his head.

I try again. "You discovered an alien signal that explains everything we don't understand?"

Xavier grins. "It's useless trying to guess. There's no way you'd guess this."

"*Shhhhh...*" Sage shushes us both as she adjusts the dial in small increments, back and forth, back and forth until—

"Hello, is anyone out there? We're over in ..." the voice cuts out into more static. "This next song goes out to ..." More static. We listen to the radio transmission for another few minutes, catching bits of words, snatches of sentences, but in the end, none of it adds up to very much.

"Okay, I'm hearing *something*, but I still don't feel scream-y. What am I missing?" I ask.

"This," Sonia says, grabbing my face and guiding my ear closer to the speaker.

I shake my head. "Okay, but I still don't—"

"Stop talking and really listen."

I shut my mouth and unshut my ears, but nope, still nada. I'm ready to declare Operation: Hear Something Scream-Worthy an epic waste of four minutes, when suddenly I ... hear it. The thing I was missing. It wasn't the DJ's voice that rendered everyone speechless—

No, there, just below the scratchy voice, tucked tightly inside the buzzy static, is the faintest of sounds. A hum. No, a drone. No, no, it's more than that.

It's ... it's ... a voice?

No way.

I'm mishearing, right?

I zero in on the mystery voice. Still, I can't make out the words. "I give up. What's she saying?" I ask.

"Listen carefully," Sonia says. "Close your eyes, block everything else from your mind, and listen."

And I do. I close my eyes and concentrate with all the focus I have. And then, slowly, slowly a pattern emerges as the words take shape. And then, with every ounce of my energy nearly exhausted, my ears straining, filtering, I finally hear it, too. The voice inside the voice buried beneath the static.

And I realize at the same time that it was Sage who'd screamed.

Because she heard the same thing I was now hearing.

The voice chanting the same five words over and over again.

Sage.

Trey.

Xavier.

Sonia.

Eddie.

Sage.

Trey.

Xavier.

Sonia.

Eddie.

Never stopping. Never breaking rhythm. But there's something else, too. Something hiding behind the crackling hum. It's the voice. It's familiar, I think. Reminds me of someone I can't quite place.

I look up at Sage, meet Sonia's and Xavier's eyes, study Trey. "Is this a joke? Is this why you guys wanted to come to the radio store? You wanted to play a joke on me, right?"

Except none of them are laughing.

I keep going, "Well, you got me, okay? I can admit it. You had me a little shook, not gonna lie. Hahaha, you guys are too much. Very funny."

Except *still* no one's laughing.

In fact, it's safe to say their four faces are the exact opposite of laughter.

Meanwhile, back on my own face, tears are starting to fill the corners of both eyes, because I know in my heart, in my bones, in my soul, this is not a joke.

It's not even joke-adjacent.

This is all-the-way, 100 percent real.

"Whose voice do you hear?" Xavier asks me.

"What do you mean *whose*? It's just a voice. Isn't the point *what* the voice is saying?"

"Our names," Sage says, nodding her head. "The voice is saying our names."

Trey clears his throat. "Only that's not even the freakiest part."

Okay, let's officially add the phrase *only that's not even the freakiest part* to our THINGS YOU SHOULD NEVER SAY TO FRIENDS UNLESS YOU WANNA SCARE THE CRAP OUTTA THEM list, yeah?

I try on a brave face. "Forgive me, but I think you're gonna be hard-pressed to show me something freakier than this."

"Listen with your heart," Sonia says. "Stop trying to figure out the voice and let the voice tell you who it is."

"Who is it, Sonia? Who am I hearing?"

But Sonia wags her head. "You know who it is. Don't be afraid of it. Don't be afraid to hear it for yourself, Eddie."

I press my ear so that it's almost on the speaker, straining to not only hear *what's* being said, but *who's* saying it. I'm nearly ready to give up when it finally hits me.

And when it does hit, when I finally hear it and recognize the voice, I nearly pass out and hit my head, if not for Trey and Xavier catching me.

I look up at my four friends and I know they've heard it, too.

"Who, Eddie?" Sonia asks. "Who's talking to you beneath the static?"

I open my lips to speak but they're trembling too hard to form the three words. The three words I thought I'd never say again.

"It's . . ."

I get the first word out, the other two stuck in the back of my throat.

"It's okay, Eddie," Xavier says. "You're okay."

I try again. "It's . . . my dad."

8500

And to think, you guys were *so* pressed to go to Trampoline Park Paradise. Ha! Bet you feel silly.

8600

The other four crowd around me closer.

Probably because they wanna hear the voice—but also maybe because as cool as this thing is, it's also kind of . . . freaky. Each of us somehow hearing the voice of someone important in their life. Even if that person isn't necessarily "alive."

I mean, guys, do you understand what's happening right now?

My Real Dad's back!!!

Is your mind blown or is that just me?

Okay, well, he's sorta back. You know, in that *disembodied voice chanting your and your friends' names and whispering gibberish out of an old, outdated radio speaker* kind of way.

But I'll take it.

Real Dad, back in any form, is the best thing that could've happened—at least for me.

I remember all those nights, when Real Dad was lying in his

hospital bed too sick to talk, how he still tried so hard to with me and The Bronster and Mom. How we could barely hear what he was saying. How sometimes we weren't even sure he was speaking real words, his pain medication making him so tired, making his brain extra foggy, so that a few times, when the nurse taking care of him asked him to verify his name and date of birth for their records, you could see his eyes flickering, feel his brain overheating, as he struggled to remember.

It's weird—maybe even ironic although sometimes I'm not sure if I'm using that word right—that this version of Real Dad, Radio Real Dad, is also hard to understand, his voice garbled and low, same as when I last heard it.

Except as excited as I am, as much as I'm trying to focus on what Real Dad's trying to tell me, I can't stop my brain from hyperfocusing on the one thing I'd rather not think about—*What if I lose him again?*

I decide the best strategy to keep Real Dad here is to keep him talking.

I ask him questions. Mostly obvious ones like, *Dude, where are you? What really happens to us when we die? Do you know what happened to Mom and the others?*

But if Real Dad knows anything, he's in no rush to share.

So far, other than the name-chanting thing—which he seems to be a huge fan of doing—the only other words I'm able to decipher are phrases I don't understand. Fragments of sentences that feel random and, well . . . meaningless.

Not that anything, anytime, with Real Dad is without meaning, that's not what I mean.

I just wanna connect with him *so bad*. How many times has something popped into my brain that I wanted to share with him? There are so many things to say to him, everything I've thought of since his funeral, things like, *I'm sorry I didn't go to the Guardians game with you back in the spring, before you got sick. If I'd known you were gonna . . . what was gonna happen . . . I wouldn't have gone to that comic book thing with Xavier and Sonia instead of hanging with you. I'm sorry, Dad. I'm so sorry.*

But also, silly stuff like, *Do you realize how much you farted in your sleep those last few days, man? Like, we were supposed to be cherishing the time we had left with you, the three of us going back and forth sharing our favorite Dad memories, and then your face would wrinkle like you were maybe having a bad dream or like you accidentally ate BURN YOUR TONGUE OFF salsa when you really only wanted MAD MILD—and the three of us would stop talking and watch you, study your face, your closed eyes and crooked mouth, but instead of you giving us some super wise gem to reflect on for after you were gone, for all the years we'd no longer have you, instead of that—you just farted. And not just any fart—no, my man, you launched a whole gas grenade. Like you just let it rip, the whole bed shaking, the small hospital room made of glass walls quickly filling up with your "internal essence" like we'd all been crop-dusted, the three of us choking, coughing, gagging on the rotten-eggs-plus-old-corn-chips fragrance, then catching the smallest of smiles curl on your lips like you knew what you'd done, as if you were saying, Hey now, no more pity parties, okay, let's save all the sad stuff for later, yeah, until we couldn't help but laugh, laugh, laugh . . .*

Eddie. Earth to Eddie. You there, man? You still with us?

I shake my head, and the hospital room melts away, taking Dad's funky butt toots with it, and I'm back in a radio supply store, with my friends who are now also kinda my family.

"Earth to Eddie. Buddy, you okay?" Xavier is asking, his hand on my shoulder.

"Huh? What? Yeah, sorry, I zoned out. I'm okay."

"You sure?" Xavier asks, his face tight with worry.

"Everything's golden," I assure him. "Any other questions we should try?"

"Ask him why we can't get to the beach," Sage suggests.

I nod but before I can get the whole question out, thick purple smoke starts pouring from outta the speaker grill and then suddenly the speaker is hotter than a hot dog in a microwave.

It's so hot that I kinda sorta . . . uhhh . . . drop it?

"Oops," I say, staring at the spot on the floor where the speaker now sits on its side.

"Oops," Xavier repeats. "You break the one thing we've got that gives us a possible connection to other humans, and all you can say is *oops*?"

I shake my head. "I didn't do it on purpose. It got sooo hot."

Sonia taps the speaker with the very tip of her finger. "He's right. If it was a person, it would definitely have a fever."

Xavier shakes his head. "That's a weird way to say it's hot, but okay."

"Maybe the battery you've got it plugged into is the wrong voltage? Wattage? I dunno. Whatever they use to measure battery power," I say with a shrug.

"Um, guys." Sonia goes pale, like she's seen a ghost again. "I didn't plug it into a battery."

"Don't be silly, of course you did," Xavier says.

Sage frowns. "It's obviously plugged into something."

"Well, only one way to find out," Trey says, and we watch him as he follows the long radio plug to the other side of the counter. "No way!"

"What is it?" Sage asks.

"What you'd find?" Sonia adds.

"More questions, that's what I found." Trey holds up the end of the cord. "It's not plugged into anything."

"But . . . but . . . it . . . it has to . . . that's not . . ." My bottom lip quivers a bit, and the words catch inside my throat. "That doesn't make any sense."

Xavier inspects the end of the cord as if Trey might've missed something, but then Sonia sets the speaker on its stomach. "Wait, there must be regular batteries inside it, duh!"

And I can't speak for anyone else but the knot in my belly, the burning in my throat, instantly relax a bit, my tense muscles loosening enough to make breathing easier.

The World's Smallest Screwdriver appearing out of nowhere, Sonia gets to work unscrewing the four tiny screws in the four corners of the battery compartment lid, her forehead furrowed in deep concentration.

And I've never watched someone open the battery compartment lid with so much interest in my entire life, and even though I hope to live many, many more years on this planet, I feel like it's fairly safe to say, I will never again watch someone open a battery compartment lid with *any* amount of interest, period.

As she twists the screw outta the fourth and last corner, everyone takes a step closer, our five heads almost close enough to bump into each other, we're leaning in so far.

"Got it," Sonia says, her fingers prying the compartment panel lid up and off and . . . and . . . and . . .

"Where are the batteries?" Sage says.

Sonia rubs her eyes like she can't believe what she's seeing. Or rather, what she's not seeing. "There . . . aren't . . . any."

Trey gasps. "What the—"

I cut in. "Okay, that doesn't make sense. Clearly, we're missing something."

Sonia nods. "Right, we've gotta be."

Xavier scratches his chin. "Well, let's review the facts. As far as we know, there's zero electricity anywhere, so how could someone even broadcast a radio signal?"

Sage bites her lip. "Unless whoever's broadcasting doesn't need electricity because they're not using actual radio signals."

Trey stares at his sister like he's just watched her unzip her alien bodysuit. "What are you even talking about? What does that even mean?"

If Sage notices her brother's concerned face, she doesn't let on. "It means, what if the signal isn't being sent by another person?"

"So then who's sending—" I snap off the end of my sentence because I realize it's not a thing I wanna finish. Apparently, everyone feels the same way, because for a solid couple of minutes no one says a single word. Not one.

In the end, it's our favorite athlete who breaks our silence.

"So what do we do? Should we try and take it home with us?" Trey asks.

Xavier stumbles, backing away from the counter, both hands up near his chest like he's telling someone to keep calm, or like he's been taken hostage and is showing he's cooperative. "No way, man. That thing's not right. I don't want it anywhere near me."

"Too dangerous right now," Sonia says. "I vote we leave it here and let it cool down."

And even though I want nothing more than to get that thing powered back on, to hear Real Dad's voice come tumbling outta that battery-less, totally unplugged speaker, I nod. "I agree with Sonia."

Sage tilts her head like she's really thinking hard, then says, "Me too."

The others echo the same.

And I don't know what makes me say it exactly, call it a hunch, a weird feeling. "Let's just make sure none of us try to sneak back over here on our own, either. No conversations with the speaker voices unless we're all here first, agreed?"

"That's probably for the best," Trey says and three nods follow.

And just like that, we're exiting the store, heading back outside, abandoning the one real clue we have, because the clue is acting like it might explode at any minute.

Which is awesome.

Totally love that for us.

8700

We're back in the car and I can't lie, I can barely buckle my seat belt, my head's spinning, my brain so buzzy. I mean, buzzing. My brain's buzzing. See what I mean?

"Soooo, are we gonna talk about what just went down or we gonna pretend like nothing ever happened?" Trey asks from the back seat.

Apparently, I'm not the only one still reeling from . . . from . . . whatever that was.

I glance across the front seat at Sonia, waiting for her to speak up, because that's what she does. She keeps us on task. Keeps us focused. She feeds us logical explanations. Which, maybe it's a little unfair, expecting Sonia to constantly make us feel better. I mean, it's just that normally she's good at it. Even when I disagree with her advice, or her theories, or her plans, I can't front—she almost always manages to convince me to see things differently, to consider another point of view. A thing I've always appreciated about her.

Especially since most of what she has to say is positive.

The bright side of things.

The silver lining.

Every group needs a Sonia. Someone who almost always throws on the lights when everyone else is convinced there's nothing but darkness.

Plus, she's a beast at video games.

But instead of hitting us with her reasonable explanation for hearing our families' and friends' voices on the radio, instead she's apparently trying her hand at the *Strong, Silent Type*.

"Well, it wasn't necessarily our families and friends," Xavier chimes in. "The voices were maybe similar but it's possible our brains were playing tricks on us. That someone was manipulating the sound. How else do you explain us all hearing someone different?"

"Isn't it possible that what we heard wasn't our families and friends at all?" I say. "What if it's some super-advanced alien race messing with us, or maybe we've all been exposed to some virus that distorts our brain waves or—or—"

"And here he is, he's finally arrived, Negative Ned in the flesh, ladies and gentlepersons," Sonia says, breaking her silence.

"Wait a minute, I'm not being negative. All I'm saying is, I agree with X. I'm not so sure that what we heard was who we think we heard. What? You don't think I want that voice to be my dad's? You don't think I'd love to think I was just inside there, listening to my dead dad talk to me? Of course. But all I'm saying is, we have to consider all the facts. There's something beyond weird going on here and I'm not ready to say I know anything for sure just yet."

"Honestly, me either," Sonia admits. "But you're still missing the point. Even if it wasn't our loved ones, we all heard *voices*. Several someones, actually. Which could mean, we aren't the only ones still out here. It means somewhere there are other people, other survivors, just like us, and all we have to do is find them and maybe, who knows, maybe they have more answers for us. Maybe they know where our families are."

"Okay, but how come I heard my dead dad?" I ask.

"You're focusing on the wrong thing here, Eddie," Sonia asserts again. "This is about us having hope that maybe we aren't alone out here after all."

"Look, I hear you. All I'm saying is maybe we shouldn't get our hopes up *too* high, you know? What if what we heard was just bad reception, or a recording from a long time ago, or . . ."

Xavier shakes his head. "Eddie, why can't you let us be excited?"

I feel my face drop a little, because I wasn't trying to be a downer. I was only trying to temper all our expectations, because I didn't want us heartbroken if that radio stuff turned out to be nothing. At the end of the day, whether we like it or not, we can't bank on people who aren't here.

REC

8800

SONIA'S KEEP IT REEL

What do I think's happened?

Hey, let me be clear up front, okay? I have *zero* clue. And honestly, right now, *what* happened isn't even the most important question.

What we should be asking ourselves is:

How are we gonna survive?

Survive *what*?

Whatever. Comes. Our. Way.

Do I think I'm being dramatic?

I don't know—would you ask me that if I were a boy, or would you call me a passionate, born leader who cares *so much*?

But yeah, okay, my theory is our town was sucked

into a cosmic event resulting in their teleportation to a parallel universe.

That also explains the voices we heard on the radio.

Including Eddie's dad's . . . because maybe that means death isn't actually being gone forever. Maybe death is traveling through time to another world. Maybe death is existing in an alternate form, in an alternate place.

8900

EDDIE'S KEEP IT REEL

Not to make everything that's happened about me, but . . . Okay, no, you know what, I *am* making it all about me, at least in this moment, at least for now, and I'm sorry but I'm not sorry. How could I be?

Because if all this . . . this . . . end-of-the-world stuff eventually reunites me with my Real Dad, well, then, maybe it's all worth it.

9000

XAVIER'S KEEP IT REEL

Listen, I get it. When it comes to what matters most right now, there are a million things that rank higher on our group to-do list. And you guys know me, do I complain from time to time? Sure, I'm only human. But also, in the end, do I always put the group first? Yep. I'm a capital *T*, capital *P* Team Player, y'all feel me?

The last thing anyone can accuse me of is being selfish . . . shoot, not me, not this guy, that ain't how I roll, ha.

I'm all team, team, and more team—that's what I'm talking about. That's what I'm about.

No doubt.

Ha.

No. Doubt.

. . .

. . .

. . .

Ahem.

But okay, I'm not gonna lie, I lowkey wish I'd heard
a barber's voice coming outta that speaker. Yo, for
real, this half-cut? Yep, it's seriously beginning to
mess with my self-respect.

It's definitely getting to me now.

Well, you know, half of me, anyway.

9100

At first glance, lunch be lunching, same as it always is.

But below the surface, the awkwardness bubbles to a boil.

"Okay, we definitely need to hit the beach now," Sage argues. "I mean, Eddie heard his *dad's voice*. Like, something's happening here."

"But we don't know *what*," Xavier shoots back. "Which is why it makes more sense to stay at camp. It's safer here."

Sonia wags her head. "I know you guys think we have enough supplies but . . ."

"I think *that's* one thing we all agree on," I chime. And it's meant as a joke, except admittedly it comes out a little hotter than intended, and Sonia nods slowly, before excusing herself from the table.

"You know how all this tension could be solved?" Sage asks.

Trey rubs his head. "Let me guess. By going to the beach."

"We're not going to the beach," Xavier snaps. "Not now, maybe not ever. So maybe just drop it."

Trey holds up his hands. "Okay, I know it's annoying but there's no need to snap at my sister."

And I expect Xavier to back down, but instead: "You know what? Why don't the two of you go to the beach and leave the rest of us out of it?"

Trey's mouth twists. "Maybe we will!"

"Cool, cool," Xavier says. "Well, it was nice knowing you two. Have fun being attacked and never making it there."

"Seriously?" Sage laughs. "How am I the bravest person here? I don't get it."

I try cutting in, running interference, but no one seems interested in what I have to say.

"Guys, how about we play a game? Or go for a swim? Or . . ."

But Xavier stomps away. "I'm out, bro. You know where to find me."

And Sage walks off in the opposite direction, Trey glancing at me like *what are ya gonna do?* before jogging after her.

9200

Over the next day, it becomes super easy to tell what matters most to everyone.

Sonia's fixated on gathering supplies because, for her money, we can never have enough batteries, or flashlights, or nonperishable foods. She makes long lists of things we need to find and then sends us on scavenging missions, moving from house to house, searching for whatever Sonia's determines is necessary for our survival.

Sage is super obvious. She's all about location, location, location.

And that location is: yep, beach, beach, beach.

Meanwhile, Xavier's sitting. In the grass in his front yard. In a lawn chair in the grass in his front yard. In a lawn chair in the grass in his side yard. Every sitting session longer than the last. He's already skipped breakfast and I'm pretty sure he's planning to skip lunch, too.

Okay, but what else is he doing other than sitting? Is he reading, singing, chanting? you ask.

"I'm meditating," he claims. "Listen, there's no way our parents, our friends, the mayor of Carterville, aren't gonna come back for us. And if we're busy going on random missions to stockpile deodorant and boxes of raisins, what if we miss them? What if they get here and we're gone, and because they're on a very tight schedule, they can't wait around for us to get back from collecting jumbo rolls of five-ply toilet paper, or from our five-mile jog around town, or our failed jet-pack ride to the beach? So, if you guys aren't gonna sit here and wait for what matters, then it's up to me to do it alone."

Which you've gotta admit is a pretty great *end-of-the-world* speech.

If we survive this whole apocalypse thing, one day we're gonna recite that speech to our grandkids.

So, with the exception of grub-time and the occasional important group discussion, we mostly leave Xavier to his yard-sitting. On the bright side, at least we know exactly where dude is at all times—which is more than you could say about the rest of us.

Then there's Trey, who's not really focused on any one thing. How does he feel about brainstorming ways to get to the beach? Um, hard pass, thanks—unless we're gonna do "sand sprints" when we make it there. *What are sand sprints*? you ask. No idea, but they sound like a special form of torture. What about supply gathering, Trey? Is he into that? Nope, not his jam ... unless you're gathering specially filtered mineral water and/or electrolyte-packed energy drinks. Oh, alpha-mega energy bars, too. Oh, and gluten-free, dairy-free, energy peanut butter. Oh, also skin-smoothing, energy serum—which, I'm pretty sure is just watery lotion. Other than that, Trey's not focused on any one thing. Unless you count physical fitness. So far, Trey spends his time shooting jumper after jumper at the park around the corner, or jogging around the neighborhood, a black plastic timer dangling from his neck to time his laps. Whenever he runs a new personal best, which seems to happen hourly, he's all smiles, all high fives and jump-in-the-air chest bumps. I can't front, his energy is mad contagious ... even if his molecularly enhanced protein bars and super-nutrient energy shakes aren't.

And as for me? On what ultra-important activity, or super-critical research, did I, Eddie Gordon Holloway, choose to devote the bulk of my personal time?

That's easy—I spent as much time as humanly possible on having ...

9300

. . . Maximum Fun.

Yep, that's right.

The way I figured, we could spend all our time worrying about what might happen (Sonia, Xavier), or trying to force things to happen (Sage, Xavier), or going well out of our way to do a little of everything (Trey)—

Or we could stop wasting precious time and look for ways to have as much fun as we could squeeze out of every single second.

After all, life's short, and I know that better than anybody. Real Dad was the funnest person ever. It's like he liked to say—

What's the point of life if you're not going to enjoy it?

So, yep, that's why I'm giving maximum run to maximum fun.

Okay, yes, I admit that was rather corny and no, that is not something I've been walking around saying before. That was the first time I've ever said it aloud, or even thought it, so—

Listen, you can't nail every motto right outta the gate.

You think whoever came up with *YOLO* dreamed it up on the first time? No way. There were probably a thousand perfectly awful sayings before they landed on YOLO. But that's the thing about these things—

Victory goes to the bold, my friends.

Which is to say, if you wanna win at life, you've gotta be willing to lose everything.

And that's me down to my bones. I'll lose all day, every day, and not think twice about it. That's how you become a visionary. That's the difference between being a person who has fun versus a person who *creates* fun. Yep, we're talking about maximizing your life's enjoyment levels. Thing is, *you gotta take a lot of L's if you're ever gonna EL-EVATE.*

Oooh, that *is* good, right? Remind me to jot that down later.

Naturally, being the fun-loving guy I am, I invite the others to join in.

"Thanks but the early bird gets the worm," Sonia replies. Which, I'm not entirely sure what that means here, but I'm assuming it's Sonia Talk for *I'm too busy gathering taller-than-Trey piles of tighty-whities.*

"Maybe after my swim?" Trey offers. "Actually, no, I'm riding my bike afterward. Definitely after that, though. Oh, shoot, no, that's my isometric training time. How about we play it by ear, yeah?"

Xavier's like, "As long as I can remain in this seat, in this grass, bring on all the fun."

And Sage is all, "You know what would be even *more* fun?"

I don't think you need to hear her answer.

"If we're gonna keep going our separate ways," Sonia says, "we should agree on a few ground rules."

I laugh because, um, I'm sorry, it is a little windy out right now, so maybe I misheard her because it kinda sounded like she just suggested we create ground rules, ha. That would be wild.

Sonia shoots me a look. "Did I say something funny?"

Wait, what?

"Um, my bad, it sounded like you were suggesting we needed rules," I say, smiling because obviously that's *not* what she said.

I follow a sudden tap-tap-tap sound down to Sonia's feet. Okay, now she's tapping her sneaker the way you do when you're all out of patience and you're trying to tell someone they really should hold all the way up. What is going on right now?!

Did she really say *ground rules*? Why is Sonia, the video game emperor, going out of her way to destroy our fun? We're supposed to be having ALL THE FUN WE CAN SQUEEZE OUT OF EVERY SITUATION.

"Rules schmools," I say, unable to control my grin. "Rules schmools," I repeat, as everyone drifts off to do their own thing. "Ha! Well, your loss, my friends! That just leaves more fun for me!"

And on one hand, it looks like I'm all alone in the Maximum Fun mission, which is a total bummer. But on the other hand, somehow we completely avoided "ground rules," so I'll take it.

Small victories, you know?

9400

XAVIER'S KEEP IT REEL

I'm not allergic to bees.

Okay, technically I am allergic. I'll break into hives, get a nasty rash, be insanely itchy. But is my life in danger? Good question. Define *danger*.

It was super dangerous when I was a kid. I'd get stung and my throat would swell tighter than two coats of paint.

But last summer, Mom had me take one of those tests where they check you for like a hundred different allergies and turns out I "passed with flying colors." That's what the doctor said, which I guess is doctor talk for "Ayyy, you won't die from a bee-sting, go crazy."

So, why did I pretend to still be super allergic?

Because everyone was so dead set on making it to the beach, they didn't care about the cost. They only cared about what they wanted. So, yeah, maybe it wasn't cool to fake out everyone like that, but since no one wanted to admit that maybe getting to the beach isn't meant to be, what choice did I have?

I want answers as much as anyone, but not if it means one of us gets injured or . . . worse. Not if it means abandoning the one place—our block—where our parents are most likely to reappear?

So judge me all you want, call me a bad guy or a jerk if it makes you feel better, but sometimes you've gotta twist the truth a bit for the greater good. All I want is for everyone to stick together and stay safe.

And look, I know everyone thinks I'm crazy for staying in this yard, but I don't care. When times are tough, we all gotta lean into what makes us feel okay, you know? And for me, it's sitting in this grass, the same grass I watched my dad cut ever since I was a little kid. I could barely walk, and I'd be wobbling after him, falling on my doopa every other foot, ha. And you know those bushes planted around the yard lamp? Me and my mom planted those together. They're rosebushes. Mom kept saying *ow* every few seconds, her hands catching those thorns, because she was too stubborn to wear gloves. So many memories in this yard. In this grass. Good memories. And when times are hard, we all gotta fall back on what we know. On what makes us feel safe. On what gives us hope.

So, yeah, I'mma keep my narrow behind in this front yard and I'mma wait it out for however long it takes. Because as long as I'm right here, I'm good.

Oh and let me address the hairy elephant in the room, because I know what you're all thinking—

What am I gonna do when I need to use the bath-room, right?

Well, that's easy, ha. I'm gonna . . . uhhh . . . I'm gonna . . . Question: Can we stop recording for a second? Yeah, let's stop because it's just weird to talk bathroom stuff, you know? Like, I totally, 100 percent have an awesome bathroom-going plan, but like, I just wasn't prepared to discuss it on camera, that's all. I mean, who *doesn't* have an awesome bathroom-going plan, amirite?

Okay, um, how about we start, uh, with the first step in my plan? You guys ready? Okay, so step number one in my awesome bathroom-going plan is—

AHGDLAKJDKLJAKLJAKFLJ!!!

A beeeeeeeee!

Are you guys seeing this? I'm in danger. Wait, you think I'm making it up, don't you? Whaaat? That's . . . that's crazy . . . sooo crazy? Yo, imagine someone pretending they were attacked by a bee? Ha!

Wow, that would be sad, right?

So. Sad.

9500

SAGE'S KEEP IT REEL

I guess y'all wanna know what I think. Suppose I see it two ways.

There's the Sage who needs to believe everyone's still at the beach. That my mom and dad are gonna pull into our driveway any minute now and Dad's gonna be all yelling down the block like, *Yo, Sage, Trey! Time to come home!* in that big booming voice, like he always does . . . while Mom pulls the hose out of the garage and walks around the house watering the lilies and roses and then when she sees me and Trey headed up the sidewalk, she'll turn the hose on us, like she always does, except she likes to pretend like she's not, like she doesn't even see us coming home so she can suddenly whirl around and spray us. Except this time we'd have Super Soaker water guns and we'd spray her right back and the next thing you know we're in a full-on water fight. We had . . . *have* a lot of those.

So, yeah, I keep waiting for things to just, I don't know, go back to normal or whatever.

But the other way it could go is we get to the beach and an alien spaceship is there waiting on us, to take us back to its home planet, where they've already taken everyone else. Or if it's not aliens, then maybe like some crazy wormhole that we'll jump into and *whoosh* tumble through time and space like a huge waterslide until the tunnel ends and we're dumped into the pool, except the pool is actually another dimension and Mom and Dad are standing there, waiting for me and Trey, and we think they're about to give us big hugs but instead they pull out two water hoses and blast us, huge smiles on their faces, all four of us cracking up as they spray us, no mercy.

9600

TREY'S KEEP IT REEL

What if they're just all gone?

Like maybe there's a mega cosmic event occurring every trillion years, and it blasted everyone on the beach into oblivion.

Or maybe it reduced them to the smallest bits of matter, so they're just floating around the atmosphere, like mini versions of themselves that are too small for the naked human eye to see. Like we'd need some supercharged magnifier or something.

Maybe the cosmic event is *still* happening and the second we finally get to the beach, the five of us will explode into neon ribbons of light, and the good news is we'll be reunited with everyone, yay!—but the bad news is we're all just floating specks of ultraviolet dust.

That or maybe we're just dead. The five of us. Maybe something happened to us, and we don't remember, and this isn't actually our real neighborhood at all, which is why no one else is here, because it's just a copy of our town meant to make our transition to the afterlife, or wherever we are, "easier," you know?

I guess that last one's kinda depressing, huh? Still, it could be worse, right? We could be completely alone, trying to figure this out by ourselves, but instead we've got each other. No matter what happens, that's something. It's something.

9700

I can't find the blue air pump.

I can't wait to venture off alone and have all my solo fun time, you know, since everyone's got their own stuff to work on, but unfortunately, I can't go until I find my blue air pump.

I nearly ask Sonia to check her inventory, but figure that joke might not land right now, so I skip it.

But why can't you use another non-blue-colored air pump, Eddie? What's so special about the blue air pump?

Excellent questions, guys, and if it's okay with you, I'd like to take the second part first.

First of all, there's nothing special about the blue air pump. It's not even one of those cool electric ones that you plug in and they're all super loud and skittering across the ground because the pumping of air makes it super vibrate-y. Nope, this thing is the kind of air pump you gotta pull up on the handle and then push down to push out the air. Then you pull the lever up again and then you push it back down again. Then you pull the lever back up again and you—

Okay, okay, you get it, sorry for wanting to make sure you guys understood what I was jabbering about—my bad, sheesh.

Secondly, here's a weird factoid: I don't know why everyone in my family always specifies "the blue" pump, because contrary to how it sounds, we have zero other pumps to speak of.

There's no yellow pump.

No red.

No purple. Or smaragdine, which is a fancy-schmancy way to say *emerald green*.

Nope. There's just . . . blue.

I guess it's one of those things where no one knows how or why a thing got started, everyone just does it because it's always been done, so you're like, welp, guess I'll do it, too.

Which, lemme tell ya, is a really great reason to *not* do it.

Meanwhile, fun fact about me: Not finding stuff I need and/or want makes me go full-on bananas.

Trust me, it's not for a lack of effort.

Nope, I search high and low—featuring a special guest appearance by Mr. Step Stool.

What, I'm a little height-deficient. My doctor said it was completely normal for a kid my age, okay?

Basically, the only place I don't search is our basement dungeon, for reasons previously explained, even if there's a decent probability The Bronster stashed it down there, knowing how much I hate that place, seeing how the only thing The Bronster loves more than farting in full elevators is making my life harder, scarier, or preferably a lot of both at the same time.

So, yeah, I limit my search party to the two non-dungeon-y floors of our house.

I search for so long the flashlight starts to flicker before finally giving out.

9800

But then I say to myself: Self, if you need an air pump, blue or otherwise, why not take your scavenger hunt on the road? Obviously, you're not the only person in Carterville history who ever needed to inflate something.

Think about it: There are soooo many inflation-thirsty things.

We're talking inner tubes, bike tires, basketballs, beach balls (ugh, let's not bring up the beach right now), soccer balls, footballs, volleyballs (okay, let's just say all the balls except tennis balls; they come pre-aired). Not to mention rafts, air mattresses, inflatable ball pits, hot-air balloons (admittedly, I'm not sure hot-air balloons use air pumps, but I need more items to make this list look legit, so).

There must be hundreds of air pumps, blue or otherwise, hanging out around Carterville, no, thousands, and all of them lonely and bored out of their mind, eager to serve, just waiting for someone to drag them out from under a bed, or rescue them from that scary dark corner in your garage, hoping to get another crack at some pumping, desperate to inflate something, anything!

Amirite?!

And you're all, *Umm, Eddie, that's what we've been trying to tell you for like the last four pages.*

True, you did hit me with that suggestion a bit ago, and I thank you for patiently allowing me the emotional space my soul needed on its personal sojourn to irrepressible truth along the road of eye-opening self-discovery and enlightenment.

Eddie?

This is he.

You know we love you, right? And we've done our best to be there for you, come what may, yeah?

Of course, guys. And I can't thank you enough for your support. It really means a lot to me.

Okay, so here's what would mean a lot to US—and we're hoping you're the guy who can help with this.

Hey, anything for you guys. Name it.

Right. So here goes: *All we want . . . is to know . . . why you need . . . a stupid air pump!*

To be fair, I never said it needed to be smart . . .

That feeling when you gotta face facts—your friends are IQists.

9900

Guys, I'm getting to the blue air pump. Just hold on a little longer, okay? It'll be worth, it, trust me. But first, we start Operation: Maximum Fun with Step #1:

Find yourself a (dope) ride.

I hop onto my bike, head-nod Xavier, and pedal north, fast and furiously, because the thing about maximizing your fun is, why waste time *not* having fun? That's right, if you're doing anything un-fun, and we do mean anything, well, then you are wasting precious MFOs.

Yep, you guessed it—

Maximum.

Fun.

Opportunities.

Please, don't let a single MFO pass you by.

And it's wild but I hear someone cheering me on.

Like they're chanting my name.

Correction: They're scream-cheering-chanting because this someone, or someones, are loud.

Anyway, I'm halfway down the street.

And that's when I realize, it's my kinda-friend.

I turn around and yep, this time it's Xavier and he's waving at me frantically, as if he is in possession of critically urgent, super important, this-can't-wait, DANGER ahead news.

So I hit a U-ey and bike back to him.

I had a feeling Xavier would come around. He wouldn't really pick sitting and doing nothing all day over having fun with his best friend. He wouldn't betray me like that!!

Why didn't you mention that earlier, Eddie, your hunch?

Um, because no one likes MR. DOES ACTUALLY KNOW IT ALL. Nope, I don't mean MR. KNOW IT ALL because when someone calls you *that*, trust me, they're throwing super shade.

Which is why I called myself Does Actually Know It All instead.

Anyway, like I said, I had a feeling Xavier would cave and come with me. Not gonna lie, I didn't think it would be this soon. I'm barely six houses down the block when he calls me back.

Still, I knew at some point, after he let his pride go, he'd have to admit the thing you and I already know.

Having fun is *waaaay* better than sitting here waiting for everyone to come back.

And it's infinitely more fun than gathering supplies like we're grizzly bears getting ready for hibernation. I mean, hello, winter's basically a full two seasons away, people!

This is midsummer! This is the time for fun! For games! For nonstop, keep-grooving-until-you-drop partying! This is The Time to Have the Time of Our Lives!

I'm just glad Xavier saw the light sooner than later; that way the two of us can get going and get this party started up rrrrrright, hahaha.

See, even my *R*'s are having fun.

And here's the deal: I don't need to hear Xavier or anyone else tell me I'm right. That's not the point. Who cares who's right (me) and who's wrong (everyone else), you know what I mean? None of that matters between friends. It's not about someone losing (everyone else) so someone else (me) can win. It's the opposite of that vibe.

More like let's all win. Because don't we all love a good *they all won happily ever after* ending? I mean, tell me if I'm wrong.

(I'm not.)

Not that it matters. At all.

(But I'm not.)

Still, I know Xavier's gonna probably feel really awful because—look, I love the guy, I do, but let's face it, sometimes he doesn't own his mistakes. He hates admitting he was to blame. It's always everyone else but him, which, ugh, who does that?

But Eddie, isn't that what you just said a little while ago?

It's not what I said. I would never say that.

But you did. You said, Who cares who's right (me) and who's—

Eh, let me stop you there. Please don't misquote me, okay? Don't. Also, just for future reference, guys, no one likes being quoted back to themselves for something they said a long time ago; it's rude, immature, and shows a real lack of compassion on the part of the person bringing old stuff back up.

But you said it like twenty-five seconds ago. That's not really the past.

You guys really love to be right, don't you?

Xavier finally reaches me, and unlike Trey he's not smiling at all.

"What uuuup, my best friend?" I ask, possibly laying it on a little too *thick*. But see, I'm trying to give my good friend here a soft place to land. Because I know he has a hard time apologizing, I'm letting him know by my tone of voice, body language, and kind facial expression that whatever happened in the past can stay there, that I've already forgiven and forgotten, because hey, that's just how I, Eddie Gordon Holloway, roll—feel me?

But any second now and Xavier will still probably drop to the grass, embarrassed by his words and actions—which I would love to remind you guys of, to keep you current, but like I said, I've already forgotten because that's who I am, I was raised right.

I'm gonna try to make this the least amount awkward as possible, so I'll probably start off my supportive, thoughtful, merciful vibes with *please*.

As in, *Please, Xavier, get off your knees, bro, c'mon man don't bow down to me, this is uncomfortable*, and then when he finally stops apologizing and begging for my humble grace, I'll stare into his eyes, into his soul, for a long, long beat before breaking out into a wide smile to let him know, *Hey, I see you. I really see you.* And then I'll say it, so he not only feels the good vibrations, he also hears the message, too. *Hey, it's okay, guys. We're all under a lot of stress. I get it. Now get on your bikes and let's get outta here, yeah?* Maybe I'll top it all off with a solid wink, sorta like, *Hey, I got you, it's all good. It's forgotten.*

You sure, just like that, it's all over? Xavier will say, worried that some of his pettiness might've rubbed off on me, which don't worry, spoiler alert, it hasn't.

And I'll reply, *What's over?*

And his eyebrows will rise and he'll be like, *Umm, the thing we were just talking about. How you were gonna extend forgiveness and also forget—*

And that's when he'll get it. When it'll finally make sense.

This is you forgetting, isn't it? he'll say.

And I'll hit him with a wink, slip my arm over his shoulders, and say, *You ready to get this show on the road, my friend?*

And he'll say, *Ha, I was born ready.*

And we'll ride our bikes off into the sunset, er. . . . the sunshine of the morning. We'll ride off into the morning sunshine.

"Will you please take a walkie-talkie with you wherever you're going?" he says, looping a walkie-talkie with a strap around my bike's handlebars like I'm three years old and always losing things. And I'm not sure how I reply but I know it sounds like *kjhadlfjldk kldahlajdhlfk agdhl.*

10000

Okay, no more interruptions.

No matter what, I will not be stopping or turning around for anything or anyone. I don't care if Sonia and Sage start sprinting down the middle of the street like Olympic track stars carrying hand-painted signs that say *PLEASE, EDDIE, SLOW DOWN AND TALK TO US WE'RE SO SORRY THAT WE NEARLY SPOILED ALL THE FUN YOU'RE RIGHT FUN TIMES ARE THE BEST TIMES AND WE'LL NEVER DOUBT THAT AGAIN, PINKIE PROMISE, OKAY?*

Sorry, I still won't turn around. I'mma still keep pedaling—even though part of me will be a little tempted to glance back because *whoa*, that's a lot of words to squeeze onto two poster boards. But even if I sneak a peek back, my mouth's staying shut. Yep, I'll let my actions talk for me.

And My Actions are like: Thanks for giving us our own voice, because while people say actions speak louder than words, we love actual words, too. We especially love poetry. Hey, maybe we can recite a poem for you. Would you like that, if we recited a poem?

ME: *Umm . . . is there a way to say no without hurting your feelings?*

MY ACTIONS: *A bit late for that now.*

ME: *Oh. Right. Sowwy.*

MY ACTIONS: *Guess we'll get back to pedaling and making you look really cool zipping down the street, while saying absolutely nothing, ever.*

ME: *I'm just not a big fan of poetry. It's nothing personal.*

MY ACTIONS: *Of course not. It never is with us, seeing how apparently you need to be a "real person" for it to be personal, and apparently "real people" only see us as a series of . . . of . . .*

ME: *Actions?*

MY ACTIONS: *Ugh, thanks, Captain Obvious, but we were gonna say activities.*

ME: *My bad. Sounded like you needed a bit of help.*

MY ACTIONS: *Hello, we're actions, not words. We walk the walk, not talk the talk. Sorry if we occasionally get a little tongue-tied, sheesh.*

ME: *Umm . . . so, uh . . . technically talking is an action, so, umm . . .*

MY ACTIONS: *Here's an idea. Why don't you try riding this bike without us?*

ME: *Ahem. Right.*

Okay, so MaxiFun Step #1: Find yourself a (dope) ride.

Well, whaddya know . . . Go-Krazy Golf & Go-Kart. How'd we end up here, haha? It's almost like it was part of Eddie's Master Plan for MaxiFun.

Ten minutes later, I'm zooming out of the Go-Krazy Pit Stop and zipping across the parking lot, every rev of the engine roaring *FUN! FUN! FUN! FUN!*

Okay, Step #1's complete.

MFO Step #2: Get a pool.

Yep, we're gonna need a pool. Preferably big enough to lie in.

And where are we gonna find a pool, Eddie?

Well, there are several pools in our neighborhood that clearly aren't being used. But for what we're about to do, probably don't wanna do that to someone else's pool. Probably best to start with a fresh, clean pool.

Um, Eddie, why are you making it sound like acquiring a whole pool is as easy as buying a candy bar?

Because it's even easier.

Watch and learn, my friends.

10100

XAVIER'S KEEP IT REEL

I think time has slowed down, or maybe even stopped completely, but like only for the five of us, and so even though it feels like it's been days since we last saw everyone, it's only been like five minutes in actual real time.

That's why I know we should just wait here because when time goes back to normal, everyone's gonna come home and we'll probably all laugh about this.

That, or like some deadly gas has spread across the country and when the military came to rescue our town they realized everyone was down at the beach and so they rounded everyone up and hid them in underground bunkers, even though our families d friends were all, *Wait, we can't leave with-out Sage, Trey, Sonia, Eddie, and Xavier*...but the military was like, *Sorry but we can't risk any more lives*. So now they're in the bunker waiting for the green light that the danger has passed. Meanwhile, the five of us are still alive because we are part of the 1 percent of the population that was born with a rare genetic trait that makes us immune to that particular strain of toxic gas, so . . . here we are, waiting. Alive and well and just . . . waiting.

That's what I think, anyway. Probably sounds stupid to you guys, I know, but it's all good. Whatever gets us through the day, right? I think the point is to keep hope. In times like this, you gotta keep hope alive. Ya gotta.

10200

I'm having so much fun, I nearly pass The Super Sports Super Store. Yep, that's really the name.

I wait for The Super Sports Super Store's doors to slide open; nothing happens.

I wave my hands near the door-opening sensor; more nothing happens.

And then I remember, duh, Eddie, there's no electricity; the door's not gonna open.

I try yanking the doors apart, but they don't budge. I'm straining and grunting and sweating down the sides of my forehead because (1) it's criminally hot out today and (2) this door is clearly very disrespectful of my plans. How selfish can you be? Blocking me from my goal. Doing your best to stand in my way.

Actually, this is perfect for our episode "NO MATTER WHAT."

I walk around to the back of the go-kart and grab a golf club.

Wait, Eddie, are you going to swing the golf club into the glass doors? After you were so against breaking into the tire shop, too?

1. No. I will not swing the club into the doors. You have my word.

2. The tire shop is a family-owned, local business. The Super Sports Super Store is a corporate chain; there are probably at least two hundred other locations, so I think they'll be okay. Besides, our Maximum Fun's on the line here; we can't let anything stand in our way.

I hop back into the go-kart and smash the gas pedal all the way down to the floor, lurching forward so quickly a box of golf balls falls off the back, the box popping open as it hits the concrete, golf balls exploding out in all directions.

The go-kart hits top speed as I stare down our target.

Yep, those sliding glass doors.

With one hand I grip the wheel and with my other hand I wedge the club onto the gas pedal, and before the kart hits the sidewalk, I hop off, losing a flip-flop in the process as I crash into the grass, my beach towel cape slightly softening my roll-landing, and I look up as the go-kart glides up the sidewalk, front tires hitting the curb, so that the kart is airborne, so that if you walked by in this precise moment, you'd think it was legit flying, as it crashes into the glass, the glass shattering into a five-thousand-piece jigsaw puzzle.

I stand up, wipe the grass stains from my knees, collect my flip-flop, and step through the broken doors as if it's perfectly normal to turn a go-kart into a battering ram.

Oh, and don't worry, with the exception of the first couple of steps, I manage to avoid most of the glass.

The Super Sports Super Store is exactly what it sounds like. A mega superstore packed with anything you could ever want or need to buy with even the slightest, most irrelevant connection to sports. Orange cones, whistles, stopwatches, bowling pins, dartboards, chalk. Yes, my friends, this is one-stop sports shopping at its finest.

10300

I'm racing past the bathrooms when I spot it.

No, not our pool.

A dark brown door that reads *MAINTENANCE CLOSET*.

Well, it actually says *MA NTEN CE CLO ET*, a few fairly important painted letters missing, chipped and peeled away to nothingness. Luckily, your boy's a beast at word games, ha!

I grab a push broom, sweep away the glass shards, and dive back into the go-kart.

Snaking through the long aisles, I scan each tall shelf.

How is there so much equipment?!

How are there so many sports?!

I brake enough to toss a few baseball bats into the passenger seat.

I speed down the badminton and water polo aisle, zoom up volleyball and cricket, and zip past gazillions of squash and racquetball gear.

But where are the pools?

Two aisles later, bingo!

One lime-green, deluxe kiddie pool covered in super-friendly animals, like dancing bear cubs, lemonade-sipping lions, Cheetos-eating cheetahs. But the majority of the plastic is dominated by grinning, top-hat-tipping giraffes. If I was gonna marry a zoo animal, it would be a giraffe because there's no shelf they can't reach, and think of how many balls they could save from rooftop rain gutters.

I drag the pool out and start blowing air in. Yes, with my lungs.

But won't that take forever, Eddie, and aren't we trying to max out our fun?

Aha! Exactly! It all comes back full circle. The Mystery of the Blue Air Pump!

I find a non-blue air pump and within seconds, the pool is taking shape. Minutes later and, why hello, there—we've got ourselves a pool.

I told you guys, stick with me, good things happen.

And now on to the next step!

Go ahead. Keep reading. I'll wait.

10400

Okay, so while you were taking your sweet time, I, Eddie Gordon Holloway, took the liberty of completing most of the next phase without you.

Trust me, you would've been bored. I did you a favor. I spared you guys an exhausting round of supermarket sweep. You owe me.

Check out our haul!

- 34 spray cans of whipped cream
- 11 spray cans of whipped topping (I'm pretty sure that's the same thing as whipped cream but I wasn't sure which to get so I just grabbed both because I'm done with grocery shopping for the day)
- 6 large bags of Haribo Starmix gummies
- 3 bottles of orange soda

- 2 bottles of fruit punch, fizzy, not flat

- 3 bottles of water

- a jar of whole cherries

- 2 squirt bottles of chocolate fudge

- 4 boxes of graham crackers

- 19 tiny containers of rainbow-colored sprinkles

- 2 candy bars

- 1 bag of chips

- 2 pairs of sunglasses

- 1 medium bag of granola

- a few random magazines

- sunscreen, the spray so we can get our own back, ha

- and last but certainly not least . . . you'll never believe what I scored . . . a large container of Triple Berry Tongue Slap Your Brain Stupid Silly Super Slushie . . . which on its own, single-handedly makes the annoying grocery store run worth it. After all, you know what they say, if you can't go to Beach Bash, you bring Beach Bash to yourself.

Who says that, Eddie?

Smart people who know stuff.

I fill the pool with whipped cream, cherries, chocolate syrup—and surround it in all the drinks and snacks, so that they're all basically within an outstretched arm's reach, and slip on my sunglasses.

I climb into the pool, careful where I step because I don't want to crush the cherries before I get to eat them.

A moment later, I'm all settled in; I'm laid out, my head resting atop an orange-squeezing orangutan—and oh yeah, baby, this is the life. Also, for once, I'm happy I'm of average height. I'm not sure Trey would fit in here, not that it matters since the only way he'd be slightly interested in this pool is if he had to lift it up with me in it and jog uphill for thirty-four miles. And if Sonia was here, forget about it, she'd probably yell at me for wasting supplies.

There's only so much whipped cream to go around, Eddie, you can't swim in whipped cream!

Um, watch me.

I grab a big yellow straw, an extra-wide one like you use for boba tea, dip the end into the whipped cream, and take a big sluuuuurrrrrrrp—

The person-sized ice cream sundae explodes into my mouth so quickly it nearly gives me a brain freeze—but instead it gives me a brain RUSH.

Ahhhh, yes. This is it. Paradise. Where I'm meant to be.

Man, I needed this. I needed to be a human milkshake. Wait, I almost forgot. I knife my hand into the creaminess, pluck out a cherry, and drop it on top of my head. Perfect.

I now officially declare this an amazing start to the best day ever.

Also, in case you're wondering, sitting in a kiddie pool filled to the brim with ice cream that the sun has already started melting to the perfect consistency?

It's like lying in a cloud made just for you.

Highly recommend it. 10/10.

But there's one key ingredient missing . . .

10500

I grab rope from the mountain-climbing aisle, loop it through the clear handle on the side of the plastic pool, and tie a knot. The other end's already secured to the go-kart. I hop in, start the engine, and a few *vroom vrooms* later, I'm back on the block in no time.

Everyone's exactly where you'd expect, doing what you'd expect.

Xavier's chilling in the grass, although now he's on a purple yoga mat, which I'm pretty sure is his mom's. Sage is lying in the driveway, drawing a blueprint for what appears to be a catapult, which, based on the pencil sketch beside her blueprint, is meant to launch her through space and over to the beach. Sonia's walking up and down the now even taller and longer rows of supplies filling her garage, one pencil tucked behind her ear, clipboard in hand as she completes her inventory. And Trey is . . .

Wait, where's Trey?

Everyone's gotta be here. I need to see everyone's face at the same time. If Trey's not here, I gotta wait. Thanks a lot, Trey. I *hate* waiting. Probably because, if you're a kid, it's the one thing *everyone's* always telling you—*wait, wait, wait*.

Well, I don't wanna. Not today. Not right now.

That's when I hear whistling and the steady slap of sneakers against the pavement.

And yep, here comes Trey, completing his late-morning jog, whistling while he works . . . out.

I drag my pool right into the center of the cul-de-sac so everyone will have to notice me.

Then I grab the duffel bag from the back of the go-kart and get busy topping off the pool's ice-cream toppings, since the heat is trying to turn my sundae into soup.

I empty a few more canisters of whipped cream (and I swear I hear Sonia cringe).

Squeeze even more chocolate syrup on top.

Rip open the small box I took from the Super Sports Super Store and remove a brand-new pair of goggles, because unfortunately, the last time I dove in, I learned the hard way you really don't want whipped cream in your eyes.

And I can tell they're trying their best to all ignore me, as if the non-fun stuff they're doing is sooo important—but trust me, once they see me fully in my human ice cream form, once they behold me in all my wonderful ice cream glory, they won't be able to help themselves. Just watch, you guys. I know my friends—sure, maybe they're a little salty right now (Sonia) but when they get a load of me, kicking back in my ice cream pool, they'll immediately stop whatever it is they're doing and race over and beg me to show them how I did it. I can hear them now:

TREY: *Oh wow, Eddie, that's so awesome! YOU'RE so awesome!*

SAGE: *You come up with THE GREATEST IDEAS! If only I was gifted with your imagination!*

XAVIER: *How could I stay in my seat when the coolest swimming pool ever is right in front of me? Move over, best buddy, I'm coming in. Cannonball!*

SONIA: *Eddie, I'm so so so sorry for being a big jerk. You were right about everything, obviously. I promise I'll never treat you that way again. Truce? Ohmigod, is that Super Slushie, too?! You really think of everything!*

And that's when I'll toss them the duffel bag and they'll be all like, *Wait, what's this, Eddie? Is there like a man-eating tiger inside waiting for us to unzip the bag so it can eat our faces off?*

And I'll laugh like, *Oh, you kids say the darndest things. Of course there's no man-eating tiger because that's sexist, guys. This tiger is 100 percent person-eating, period.*

And then, understandably, they'll be a little afraid to open it, and I'll have to promise that it's nothing bad inside, I'll have to swear on my highest *Dragon Insurgents III* score or something to prove I'm not lying, and then finally they'll unzip the duffel and they'll pull out the four identical packages, all gift-wrapped of course by yours truly, with a bow on top because c'mon, you've gotta have a bow—and they'll rip open the presents like it's X-mas in July, and the looks on their faces when they see what's inside—

Four inflatable swimming pools, just like mine.

And once they're done crying happy tears of indescribable joy, I'll present them with the air pump like, *Hiii, ice cream social, anyone?*

This is gonna be so good! I've had some good ideas in my day, but this one takes the cake—the ice cream cake, that is.

Groan, Eddie.

Sorry, I had to. Now, if you'll excuse me, guys, it's time I get this party started! I walk about ten feet away from the pool and then, with my goggles locked and loaded, I race toward the ice cream, leap into the air, tucking my legs, smiling, laughing, as I disappear into a cloud of perfectly whipped cream.

10600

Fifteen minutes later—

Okay, so no one has come over to the ice cream pool yet, they're still fighting to resist me, but I can feel their willpower weakening. Any minute now and they'll cave, just you watch. Patience, guys, patience.

Eighteen more minutes later—

Okay, well, things are admittedly starting to really melt but no worries, we've still got plenty of refreshments to top things off with, so as long as they all head over here in the next thirty minutes we'll still be golden, haha. Can't wait!

Nineteen more minutes later—

I admit, I'm a little worried no one's coming. Maybe they don't see me? Could that be it? No, that's not possible. I was saving the second part of my plan as a surprise, but I think now is actually the perfect time. I pull the boom box from the back of the go-kart, pop eight new C batteries inside, turn the volume to the max, and push play—

And *boom*—now our party's got bass-bumping, speaker-rattling summer jams and no one can resist a great beat, amirite?! You can be mad as all get-out but let someone pop on some tunes—it could be a song you don't even like, but you can't help yourself, see if you don't start bopping your head, tapping your foot. Hahaha, secret weapon activated! Sorry, guys, I didn't want to have to pull out the big guns so soon, but you left me no choice.

And within five minutes, while I'm chomping down a hand-ful of maraschino cherries, here comes Sonia, walking down her driveway, headed straight for the ice cream pool party.

Part of me wants to make her work for my forgiveness because she really didn't have to be so mean to me for just wanting to have a little fun, but I'm not gonna be a jerk. When someone apologizes with their heart, the least you can do is accept it with your own.

"Hey, you," I say, reaching for the duffel bag with the wrapped presents inside. "Here for the par—"

But Sonia walks right past me and the duffel bag, over to the boom box, turns the volume down so much the rattling bass sound is reduced to a raspy whisper. She doesn't even look at me, just walks right past me again, back up her driveway, and back into the garage, pulling the rope handle behind her, the garage door dropping shut in a low thud.

I catch Xavier staring at me, but he quickly looks away.

In the end, Trey's the only one who comes over. "That looks like fun, Eddie. Having a good time?"

"WHAT'S THAT, TREY? AM I HAVING A GOOD TIME?" I repeat, way louder than necessary, so that my voice carries all over the cul-de-sac for everyone to hear me. "I'M HAVING THE VERY BEST TIME OF MY LIFE!"

Trey makes a concerned face. "You okay, man?"

"Huh? Yeah, I'm cool. Just living the good life, jamming to this summer soundtrack I found at one of the stores I explored earlier."

"Yeah, okay," Trey says, staring at me the way your mom does when she's not convinced you're actually fine. "Do me a favor? Maybe take a break from the sun for a bit, yeah?"

But before I can reply, Trey's jogging the other way.

10700

SAGE'S KEEP IT REEL

Did part of me wanna dive into that ice cream sundae? Duh. Ice cream drizzled in chocolate sauce and topped with mountains of whipped cream? I'm not ashamed to admit a couple drips of drool fell onto my blueprints. I'm only human.

But you think I was about to give Eddie that satisfaction? Ha. Not today. Not. Today.

Besides, the only whipped thing I care about right now is me . . . being whipped through the air in this catapault. Beach, here I come!

I just need a few more tweaks to the design because currently, if my calculations are correct, it'll launch me over the beach and into the middle of the lake.

10800

So the ice cream sundae plan didn't work as well as I envisioned.

But don't worry, we're just getting started.

Operation: Lure Back Friends is on and poppin'.

Eddie, has anyone ever told you sometimes you sound like a thirty-something-year-old man who spent the first two decades of his life living in a medium-sized northeast Ohio suburb?

Was it the "on and poppin'"?

It didn't help.

Well, then, how 'bout we get back to our mission? I have a good feeling we're gonna get this thing turned around.

That sounds nice, Jrue, but honestly the odds you'll turn things around seem . . . well, how can we say this without hurting your already weakened self-esteem? Um, how about super low?

Sheesh, nothing's turning around with *that* attitude. How 'bout saying something positive?

Sorry, Eddie, you're right.

Umm, duh.

We are positive *the odds of you turning things around are super low.*

See? You're positive. Was that so hard?!

Phase Two of Operation: Lure Back Friends is simple.

Make sure whenever my friends see me, I'm always in the middle of experiencing an amazing MFO.

For example, later in the morning, when Xavier finally leaves his grassy post to go potty, I make sure that on his way back, he spots me cracking up laughing. Like, I'm cackling, I'm laughing so hard. Slapping my knee, doubled over trying to catch my breath, beads of sweat rolling along my forehead, I'm laughing so hard. Naturally, he can't help but take a peek back at me, wishing he was also experiencing that unrelenting force known as COMEDY.

Except when he finally caves and asks, *What's so funny?* I can't remember the joke I told myself, so instead I shake my head and rub my belly like, *Sorry, buddy, but I'm too busy yucking it all the way up.*

Like I said, easy peasy.

Trey's a little tougher to crack, but I know if I'm gonna win him over, I'm gonna need to choose something fun *and* athletic. So I wait until he's heading out for his morning jog, and then race ahead, lying down in the middle of the road. Just as I hear him coming toward me, I spring to action, sitting up at the waist and falling back down to the street. I repeat this process several times until, winded and out of breath, I stay fallen down.

You mean you do sit-ups?

Whatever. Moving on, for Sage, I accidentally leave out a thin stack of hand-drawn blueprints that just so happen to show you exactly how to build a human cannon. I even make up a math problem that shows how fast you'd need to launch to make sure you landed in the beach sand, and not smack-dab in the middle of Lake Erie. Then, to top things off, I tape a sign on the outside of the garage door that says *PLEASE DO NOT ENTER. OPERATION: BLAST TO THE BEACH IS CURRENTLY UNDER CONSTRUCTION. AUTHORIZED PERSONNEL ONLY.*

And finally, I spend a couple of hours researching "Best Ways to Organize Your End-of-the-World Supplies" at the library, walking out with an armful of books that I start reading out loud while sitting in a random spot on the lawn that coincidentally is within earshot of Sonia's ever-expanding supply depot.

But, alas, I'm sad to report that although their faces light up at the sight of my endeavors, either no one's curiosity gets the best of them, or they're genuinely so distracted by their own pursuits that they don't even notice the bait I set for each of them. Yep, despite my best efforts, all four of my friends resist my sincere attempts at engagement . . . and just like that, Operation: Maximum Fun remains a solo mission.

Still, if they think I'm gonna let them rain on my fun parade, well, they don't know Eddie Gordon Holloway, ha! Because the thing about me? I have fun no matter who I'm with, no matter what I'm doing, even when my only company is me. Plus, I hear Mom's voice bouncing around my brain like, *Eddie, if you're bored, that's your own fault. There's sooo many awesome things you could be doing.* And yeah, just because I hated when Mom said stuff like that because boredom isn't always your own fault, because sometimes it's actually your boring friends' fault, doesn't mean there's not some truth to Mom's words. Besides, the way I see it, I can either give in to the boredom and let it wear me down into oblivion, or I can stare Boredom in its dark, soulless eyes, and say, *Not today, Boredom. Not this guy.*

And I'm pretty sure it goes without saying which path I pick, amirite?

I mean, you guys know how I roll.

But yeah, uh, just in case, it's the second one. I choose Door #2.

Yep, that's right, I look Boredom dead in its eyeballs, and I stare Boredom down, down, down.

I stare it down so bad it's more like, um, Boredom, or Boredown?

BAHAHAHAHAHA—HA HA HA HA ha . . . ha.

Whatever, it was funnier in my head, I don't care if you laugh.

Anyway, I have so many fun solo ideas, I have to scribble them in a notebook so I don't forget any. Look at this list, there are some classics on there, if I do say so myself.

EDDIE'S LIST OF AWESOME ALONE (BUT NOT LONELY, AT ALL) ACTIVITIES:

1. A coloring book except instead of using crayons or colored pencils, you use kitchen condiments like ketchup, mustard, and Thousand Island dressing. Is it messier than traditional coloring tools? Yes, yes, it is, but that's part of the fun! The messier the better, amirite, friends?! Plus, this way, your artwork's completely edible, which is perfect because creating so many masterpieces works up your boy's appetite!

2. A footrace where you race . . . yourself. Admittedly, this idea's got a few bugs to work out before it's ready for prime time, but think about it, how many races have you ever lost to . . .

yourself? Yep, you're definitely winning, hahaha. That fool you're racing against doesn't stand a chance!

3. Write a book. Ever wondered what to do with all those brilliant, fully developed story ideas trapped inside that creative skull of yours? It's simple. Write a novel . . .

4. Okay, turns out writing a whole novel takes more than thirty minutes, so I'm adding point four as an alternate option. Yep, number four is write a short story. That's right. It's like a novel only awesomely shorter.

5. Okay, turns out writing a short story also takes more than thirty minutes, so I'm adding point five as an alternate option to suggestion four. Write a poem. That's right. It's like a short story only even shorter.

6. Okay, I'm not gonna bore you with the whole thing again, but yeah, feel free to reduce your poem to a haiku.

7. Okay, bump the haiku. Poetry's stupid, anyway.

8. Enter an eating contest. This can be hot dogs, cookies, or hot wings. That's the beauty of this activity, the food options are limitless! Plus, the same rules and advantages we created in Suggestion #2 also apply here. That's right, you can totally take your time if you want, because digestion is clutch, and you can still win the contest! Eating at your own regular

pace in an eating contest?! Truly mind-blowing! An utter game changer! Who came up with this awesomeness, that's what I wanna know, because frankly, I'd love to meet that person. And I'd also like to shake their hand and say, *Hey, I know we don't know each other, I know we're perfect strangers, but somehow I feel like we're super connected, you know. Anyway, I just wanted to tell you, and I'm sure you get this all the time, you're so incredible. Your ideas are flawless. I mean, brilliant! In the span of a single afternoon you single-handedly created not just one cure for boredom, but EIGHT AMAZING, INDIVIDUAL cures. Bravo, you perfect stranger who I definitely don't know nor have I ever seen you before in life until just now . . . bravo.*

10900

EDDIE'S KEEP IT REEL

Guys . . .

I'm . . .

I'm so . . .

Guys, I'm so bored! I can't keep doing this! Coloring with condiments? Yeah, not as fun as it sounds. I knooowww, surprising, right? You'd think sweet relish would give you a richer green, but nope, all it does is wet your paper and tear holes in it. Like, c'mon, dude, really? Seriously, don't waste your time, guys. Plus, it makes your hands smell like sugary pickles. It's super dumb.

But you know what's even dumber?

Hanging out by yourself.

Dumber and boringer.

Ohmigod, guys, I just said boringer.

What's wrong with me?!

I'm not built to be alone. I need my friends back. I don't care what it takes.

I can't survive like this.

I mean, why would you even want sugary pickles in the first place? I would've loved to be at that creative meeting.

BOSS: *Okay, well that concludes our meeting unless anyone has anything else they wanna add?*

EMPLOYEE: *Oooh, oooh, guys, check this out, best idea ever . . . picture pickles, okay? You got it? You picturing pickles in your head? Okay, now sprinkle sugar on 'em.*

BOSS: *Umm, well, thanks? I'm not sure what to say, to be honest.*

EMPLOYEE: *Um, try thank you.*

BOSS: *Huh? No, your idea's ridiculous. Why would I . . . thank you?*

EMPLOYEE: *You're welcome.*

BOSS: *No, see, I'm not thanking you. I'm saying, Why would I thank you?*

EMPLOYEE: *Again, you're welcome. And thank you for your attention. It's sooo hard being a visionary, you know? Wait, what am I saying? Of course, you don't know.*

Ohmigod, guys, it's worse than I thought. I'm so bored I just wrote a play and acted out both sides. I mean, was my performance both brave and inspiring? Yes. That goes without saying. But could it also quite possibly be a cry for help?

Yes.

I'm crying and I need help.

Please, guys, I'm begging you, send help.

There's no time to waste. Right now the boredom's contained but if this thing were to get out and be exposed to the human population, well, things could quickly escalate beyond anyone's control.

So, if you don't wanna watch what's left of humanity die an agonizingly slow and painful death, you know what to do.

Send. Help. Now.

11000

Okay, so can I be honest with you now?

Not that I want to add anything to your plate, not that I want to add my worries, concerns, problems, fears to your plate—

But I know right now, if I keep this stuff locked inside me, I'm gonna lose it.

I need to get this thing off my chest, yeah?

If I said I haven't been a little nervous the last couple of days, like a little anxious, I'd basically be lying through my teeth, because yeah, I'm definitely feeling a lot of complicated feelings right now, because yeah, here we are.

Everyone is really gone. This is really a thing.

Hey, can I be extra, ultra honest for a sec?

There are times when I actually . . . when I . . . wow, this is so hard to say, I'm sorry . . . Okay. Okay. Let me try again.

There are times when I actually *wished* my family disappeared.

Even back when Real Dad was still here. When Real Dad was still alive.

There were times when I'd be so frustrated, so angry, so hurt by something that Mom, Real Dad, or The Bronster had said or did to me, that in my heart—never out loud, thankfully—I WISHED WITH ALL MY MIGHT, WITH ALL MY WISHING POWER, that I'd wake up and The Bronster would just be . . . gone.

That Real Dad or Mom, or Real Dad and Mom, would go to work and just not . . . come home. And okay, you're like, *Okay, Eddie, but we've all wanted to be home alone sometimes, who doesn't wanna have the house to themselves sometimes, who doesn't wanna do what they want, eat what they want, stay up as long as they want, wear what they want, basically do whatever they want whenever they want for however long they want—*

Who wouldn't want that, at least sometimes?

And yeah, you're right—

Except I didn't just want my Home Alone, no-more-rules, megaparty—

(I mean, I didn't *not* want that, too, but . . .)

No, I was angry and frustrated and I wanted *new* parents, *different* parents, because I didn't like mine sometimes. Not because they're awful, or terrible—most of the time they were fine, and a lot of times they were awesome even—

But there were days and nights when I'd be mad because Mom was in a bad mood, or because she wasn't being fair, like maybe instead of hearing my side and understanding how cool my laundry plan was, she'd be all *No, Eddie, I'm not gonna listen to whatever wild thing you've dreamed up this time, just please do what I'm asking you, just do what I'm telling you, okay, because like it or not I'm Mom, I'm the parent, and I'm responsible for you, and you're not gonna like everything I do or say, but at the end of the day, that doesn't matter, because at the end of the day I expect you to be obedient, to follow the rules, even the ones you disagree with, no, especially the ones you disagree with and honestly I don't wanna hear why you think I'm wrong, or why you think you don't think the rules apply to you, or whatever else you dream up—sometimes I just want you to do the thing I tell you, without complaining or arguing or trying to convince me otherwise, okay?!*

Which, I get, kind of.

But also, it wasn't fair that just because she's an adult, just because she's my mom, that she *always always always* got to have the last word on *everything*.

So yeah, sometimes, when I'd be hanging out at Sonia's and her parents were cooking her favorite dinner not for any special occasion but just because, or when Xavier's dad would pick us up from school and drive us straight over to Trampoline Park Paradise to get our jumbo trampoline life on just because he wanted to see Xavier (and me) happy, I'd think to myself, *I wish you were my parent instead.* Can you believe that, guys? I'd actually say to myself, *Man, how much better would life be if I had these parents instead of mine?*

And again, this was before WBD was even in the picture.

This was when Real Dad was alive. And not just alive, but when Real Dad wasn't sick. When Real Dad and Mom were still very much alive and very much together and very much in love with each other, I *still* wanted something different.

Okay, sure, that's a lot, Eddie, and thanks for sharing it all, but, uh, what exactly are you saying? Why are you telling us all this?

I'm telling you all this because . . .

Because there's a part of me that maybe possibly definitely wonders thinks knows that it's my fault.

That I'm the reason why everyone's gone.

That this is because I wished for this.

I was mad that morning and while I didn't say it out loud, or say it to you guys, inside I was definitely wishing Mom and WBD and everyone would just be not . . . here.

I didn't care where they went.

And if I'm being real, I didn't care *how long* they'd be gone.

I wasn't being picky.

I just wanted them gone.

And I promise you that ever since I realized that maybe they weren't coming back, I've done nothing but hope and pray and beg and plead inside for my wish to be reversed, for my wish to be undone, for whoever worked in the Secret Wishes People Make department (wherever it was in the universe) to let me take back everything I said.

Because as much as I wanted Beach Bash, I didn't want it like this.

So, you see, everything that's happened, everything that's gone wrong, all of it, it's all my fault. I'm the one to blame. Me. Me. Me.

It's all me.

And so it has to be me who brings them back.

I owe that to them. I owe it Sonia and Xavier and Sage and Trey, too.

It's all on me.

And somehow, someway, I've gotta make it right—first with my friends, and then, with any luck, hopefully one day soon, with everyone else.

But how do I make it right?

If only there was somewhere I could go for great advice . . .

11100

I hop outta the go-kart and push open the front door of the radio store.

And it's right where we left it, which shouldn't be a surprise, why wouldn't it be? Except part of me half expected to walk down this aisle to the back of the store and find it . . . missing.

But the thing about Real Dad? Even when he can't actually be here, he still finds a way to be here for me when I need him the most.

"Hey, Dad," I say, picking up the speaker box and holding it up to my ear. "What's new?"

And I'm not gonna lie to you and suggest suddenly my Real Dad's voice boomed from the radio grill, loud and clear. It's still mostly impossible to understand. But there is one new word I manage to pluck from the transmission:

Leak?

Hmm, interesting choice. Dad, what are you trying to tell me?

Leak.

I don't get it.

I hold the radio back up to my ear, listening carefully for the new word.

There it is again . . . *leak.*

Lea—

Hold on.

Wait a minute . . . I don't think it's *leak.*

No, I think Dad's actually saying . . .

Lead.

As in be a leader, Eddie.

Set the example.

Be better than you've been.

As in, it's not so much what comes outta your mouth, those are just words, but more about the things you do and the actions you take.

Lead, Dad says, and his timing couldn't have been better.

"Thanks, Dad," I tell him.

And once again, purple smoke starts pouring from the radio, and suddenly it's too hot to hold.

But this time, as I carefully set it back down atop the counter, I wonder if that's not also Real Dad trying to tell me something.

Something meaningful like, *Love can either warm you up, or it can burn you into oblivion. Either way, it's worth it, Eddie. It's worth it.*

Or you know, the heat could just mean there's a short in the radio's wiring and I'm reading way too deeply into a largely empty experience.

But like I said before, y'all already know how I roll.

Yep, I'mma go with Door #1.

Because everything that we're going through right now, the good, the bad, and ugly, it all has to mean something, right? Something important's gonna come outta all this, yeah? Which means, all we have to do is push through, lean on each other, and survive.

Because no matter what, it's worth it, guys.

11200

And boom, OPERATION: BEST APOLOGY EVER is underway!

And it starts at the party supply store.

I'm loading boxes of confetti onto the go-kart when I notice the store next door—BEST PETZ.

When I was little, I begged Mom and Real Dad to take me there all the time so I could pet the puppies, secretly hoping Mom would fall in love with them so hard that she'd forget all about her mild allergy to fur.

I even had a name picked out and everything. *Cheeto.*

What? I loved cheese curls, and I was eight, give me a break.

Except there's something not quite right about BEST PETZ right now, other than the fact that it's so dark inside. And then it hits me: The animals are probably hungry, with no one around to feed them. I try the front door and it's locked. But when I drive around to the alleyway, luckily, the rear door isn't. Sure, I could've just used the golf-club method and broken the glass, except I didn't wanna risk any shards flying into the cages or tanks.

It's even darker in the back of the store because there are no windows, and after snapping on my flashlight, I realize I'm in the stockroom, surrounded by stacks and stacks of pet food, pet toys, beds, snacks, collars, leashes, and every other thing necessary to keep your family pet happy.

I step through the aisle, careful not to trip over any boxes, until I make it to two swinging doors with a sign taped on one side that says *Main Floor.*

Bingo.

I start to push through the doors but then I change my mind and race over to one of the shelves, pulling down a jumbo bag of puppy chow. First I'll feed the pups, then I'll make my way around to the birds, the fish, the kittens, and ugh, even the snakes—I hate snakes.

This time I step through the swinging doors, dragging the puppy chow behind me, and a little excited about all the puppy love I am about to be surrounded with.

"Lunchtime, guys," I say as I let go of the bag and aim my flashlight at the closest animal station—and voilà, there's the fish alcove, aka thirty or so glass tanks stacked in columns of three, filled with every variety of fish you could think of.

Except . . .

I walk deeper into the alcove, and the closer I get to the tanks, the brighter my flashlight illuminates the rows of glass. And I nearly drop my flashlight because this . . . this doesn't make sense. I quickly look in every single tank, and every time it's the same thing.

I know what you're thinking, *Please don't tell us the fish are dead, Eddie.*

No, the fish are not dead. At least I don't think. I guess I don't actually know because . . . because the fish are . . . gone. I double-check every tank, this time really taking my time, and there's nothing there, not even a single guppy.

Which is weird because all the tanks are filled with water and pebbles and all the normal decorative fish tank stuff. Just without the fish.

And then a scary thought bursts into my brain and suddenly I'm leaving the fish alcove and sprinting toward the puppy cages—

And my worst fears are confirmed—all the puppies are gone, too.

Same with the cats.

The birds.

The rabbits.

The mice.

The hamsters.

The frogs.

The lizards.

Even the snakes.

Someone took the snakes. The pet store's been robbed.

Who would rob the pet store?!

And who would *want* all the pets? I mean, you've seen one ger-
bil, you've seen a hamster, amirite?

And that's when another thought hits me. In the days since
everyone's disappeared, we haven't seen any animals except—

Wait, did you hear that?

There's somebody in here. Back in the stockroom.

I snap off my flashlight and tiptoe over to the swinging doors,
pushing one open slightly—and sure enough I can just make out
someone on the ground, their head bobbing, and they're breathing
so hard—I aim my flashlight and power it back on, the light will
blind them, and I'll have the upper hand, right?

"Who are you, intruder? And what did you do with all the pets?"
But the intruder doesn't answer, and with my flashlight beam
reflecting off the metal cages, I've actually blinded myself. "What's
the matter, cat got your tongue?" I ask, because I'm corny, fight me.

That's when they suddenly leap up and head right for me, their body hurtling through the air, knocking me to the ground, sending my flashlight flying into the corner and throwing us both back into darkness.

I try to fight them off me but they're way too heavy.

This is the end, I think to myself. The Best Petz Bandit is gonna get rid of me so I don't expose their thievery. "Don't worry," I assure them. "I won't tell anyone I saw you here, okay? Your secret's safe with me, just don't hurt me."

I feel their hot breath move from my neck to my face and, *gulp*, I know this is it. This is officially the end of Eddie Gordon Holloway, and while being eaten alive by a monstrous pet burglar is certainly not the ending I would've chosen, I just want you all to know it's been a blast getting to know you. Seriously, an absolute treat. Farewell for now, maybe our paths will cross again in the next life and—

SLRRRRPPPPP!

Wait a minute, did The Best Petz Bandit just lick my face?

SLRRRRPRRRRPPPPP!!!

Okay, so yes, licking's confirmed . . . unfortunately.

And then The Best Petz Bandit makes a sound that I'll never forget. A sound that nearly makes my soul exit my body.

11300

"WOOF, WOOF!"

And yep, I recognize that bark anywhere. "Mr. Bubbles?!"

"WOOF, WOOF!" Mr. Bubbles says, his super-slobbery tongue headed right for my face, again. *SLRRRRPPPPP!*

And I'm so happy to see him, I'm only grossed out a little bit.

~~~~~

Me and Mr. Bubbles spend the entire rest of the day setting things up.

Well, *I* spend the rest of the day setting things up.

Mr. Bubbles drags his water bowl under the shadiest tree in the yard and takes a nap.

Yep, while I place all the orange plastic cones in the grass, up and down the hillside, Mr. Bubbles is snoring like he's in the semifinals of The Planet's Loudest and Most Obnoxious Noises competition.

I'm hammering wooden stakes into the grass and stringing

ropes around each one when Mr. Bubbles suddenly appears at my side with a red ball in his mouth . . . along with a mouthful of dog slobber.

I shake my head. "Sorry, Mr. Bubbles, but I'm not touching that ball. No way. It looks like you've been marinating it in an overnight slobber sauce, my guy."

Mr. Bubbles wags his head and his tail like he's preparing for liftoff—and okay, I'm a sucker for enthusiasm, so I track down a non-contaminated ball to throw him, waving it above his head before launching it across the yard. And I think to myself, *Wow, I'm pretty good at this dog-caring stuff. And Mom said I'm not responsible enough. Ha!*

Only Mr. Bubbles doesn't chase after the ball.

Mr. Bubbles doesn't move.

Even his tail stops wagging.

"What's up? I threw it already. Go get it, Mr. Bubbles."

But Mr. Bubbles nudges that slobbery ball against my knee and I nearly leap into Pluto's atmosphere. "Eww, Mr. Bubbles. Sorry, bruh, but I'm *not* throwing that ball. Nope. No way."

I fold my arms across my chest and turn my back to him so he knows I mean business.

But from the corner of my eye, I can see he won't drop it . . . literally.

"Fine," I say, giving in. "BRB."

I search the garage first but finally find what I'm looking for in a kitchen drawer.

Back outside, I smile triumphantly at Mr. Bubbles and hold out my plastic-gloved palm.

"Okay, dude, how 'bout now?"

And I swear Mr. Bubbles smiles, the super-saturated ball plopping into my hand, slobber splashing everywhere like when you jump in a puddle.

"But look, we can only do this for a few minutes, okay?"

Mr. Bubbles makes a sound that sounds like a laugh.

I shake my head. "For real, man. Only a few minutes. I've got a lot of work to do and since *someone's* not interested in helping, I've gotta do it solo, so . . ."

But as uninterested as Mr. Bubbles is in helping, he's even less interested in hearing me talk about helping, so I just throw the wet ball across the yard, Mr. Bubbles taking off after it, happy and worry-free.

A full hour of throwing and fetching later, Mr. Bubbles and I are settled in under the shady tree, his big tongue lapping up water from his bowl while I chomp on peanut butter crackers and gulp my own water.

After our break, I try to get Mr. Bubbles to come with me back to work, but nope, my man, slobber ball back in his mouth, immediately runs in the opposite direction—which honestly, can I blame him??

It's exactly what I used to do whenever I sensed Mom was about to hit me with another chore.

Welp, guess I'll see ya later, Mr. B.

Minutes later, I manage to find five burlap sacks and I leave them in the tall grass near the garden.

I stop off at Go-Krazy Golf & Go-Kart and find the keys to the rest of the go-karts, driving five of them one by one back to the Johnsons' house.

And before you ask who are the Johnsons and why are you in their house, the Johnsons are super rich. Like filthy rich. It's arguably the best house in all of Carterville.

So you're saying you're taking advantage of the Johnson family's disappearance to hang out at their house, Eddie?

Um, duh.

I go to the hardware store and find the biggest tent tarp I can find, only to realize when I get it back to the house that it won't work. So then I drive back to the hardware store and find the biggest *white* tent tarp I can find and take that one back to the house, and this time it's perfect. I drag five beanbag chairs up from the Johnson family rec room and set them up on the lower deck in the backyard.

I go to Sally's Salon and after realizing there's no possible way to get what I need through the door—no matter how I try to angle it, it just won't fit—I tie a heavy metal chain around it, the other end already secured to the go-kart, and I gun the engine, zooming across the parking lot until the chain goes taut and the big glass window bursts into a million beautiful pieces, as the thing I came for sails right through. It's too big to throw on the kart, so I hoist it onto a dolly with wheels and tow it back to the house.

And last but not least, I mosey back over to Party Planet, the only party supply store in town, and I race up and down the aisles, tossing everything I need into a shopping cart. Five stuffed shopping carts later, I cross off the final item on my checklist. Mission accomplished. I use the metal chain to secure all five shopping carts—and then it's back into the go-kart, the caravan of shopping carts rattling behind me like whiny metal cattle.

It takes hours to decorate. I hang party streamers. There's pin the tail on the donkey. I "bake" cakes on the grill—because yeah, I could've just picked up a few from the bakery, but those are a few days old now and I really wanna show everyone I'm serious about all this, that every bit of it is from my heart.

I'm smacking the final piece of tape onto the hanging banner when it hits me hard.

Sheesh, I'm exhausted.

But, as I look at all the stuff I did, I can't hide my excitement. I can't stop smiling because am I beyond tired? Yes. And was it worth it? One hundred percent. No matter what, it was all worth it.

The final and arguably the most important piece to this whole thing I do sitting out on the deck, in one of the super-comfy lounge chairs.

I uncap the fancy pen I found in Mrs. Johnson's home office, and I get busy.

The moon's out and high in the sky by the time I pull back up to camp on my bike—I left the go-kart in the Johnsons' garage, charging on their generator—geez, what didn't that family have?!

As I expected, everyone's already asleep, which is just as well considering it might've been awkward if they'd said *no* right to my face. This way, no one gets hurt. At least not directly. There are four envelopes in my hand, with one name written on the front of each.

I move my way around the tents, propping an envelope up next to each sleeping bag, and for a moment, right before I dip out, I consider sleeping at camp, being close to my friends for the night, but I stick to the plan, and zoom away.

Even before my face hits the ridiculously comfy pillow in the ridiculously comfy king bed in the ridiculously awesome master bedroom, I'm already passed out, ZZZZ's and dreams coming fast and hard.

11400

I wake up feeling more refreshed than I have in a while.

I take a long, hot shower—shout-out to the Johnson family generators making my dreams of hot water a reality.

I toss my ADHD meds into my mouth and—hold up. Pro tip for those of you who don't like taking pills because you struggle to get them down: That used to be me, too, until my doctor hipped me to leaning my head *forward* instead of tilting it back, which, I know, I know, seems like that wouldn't make sense, but I'm telling you, it works!

(Shout-out to Dr. Liz!)

I chase the pills down with a big gulp of spring water. I don't know what it is about drinking out of a bottle that makes me wanna say *ahhhh* after every sip.

Like if I didn't make a point to *not* say ahh and I just let things happen naturally, I would for sure be punctuating every sip with *ahhh*, which, while I would never presume to speak for you guys, but as my good friends I would assume you'd not say a word to me—you'd just snatch the bottle from me and fling it to Antarctica, because no one wants to hear *ahhh* after *every* sip. Six or seven sips, maybe. But not every or even every other. It also depends on how much time you're taking between sips—sip frequency would definitely factor in, too.

I gobble down a bagel, gulp down some oat milk—don't look at me, it tastes better when WBD's not here to force it down your throat, and no not literally; gosh, guys, he's an environmentalist, not a monster.

I clear yesterday's letter-writing paper and envelopes from the table, rereading the final draft I'd written on notebook paper before carefully, painstakingly transferring it onto four different pieces of fancy stationery.

> *Dearest Friends,*
>
> *I understand I haven't been my best self these last couple of days and I am sincerely sorry for the way I've acted. We've all been through a lot and it hasn't been easy for any of us. My therapist says that when people are under stress, we all react differently. We all have different ways of coping. I'm*

sorry for acting like my way of coping—having nonstop fun

so that I didn't have to think about how afraid I was—was

the only way to deal with things. I respect, admire, and

appreciate each one of you and I can't imagine being here

with any other friends. As a small token of our friendship,

I have a surprise for each of you. Therefore, I humbly

request your presence at the Johnson family house—you

know, the over-the-top megamansion on the hill—at 12 noon.

I hope to see you there, but even if you decide not to come, I

hope you still accept my apology and find it in your hearts to

forgive me.

Sincerely your friend forever,

Eddie G. Holloway

Maybe it's a little too formal, I think, but hopefully, they can tell I really mean every word of it. Hopefully, they forgive me. But that's not up to me. All I can do is apologize and try my best to do better. To be better.

I check my watch—11:13 a.m.

And now there's only one thing left to do.

I grab a book from the massive Johnson family library, park myself on the porch steps, crack open my book, and wait.

11500

At 12:11 I know they're not coming.

Sonia is a stickler for being on time for things, and from what I can tell, Trey and Sage are, too. *Welp, Eddie, you tried*, I think to myself. *You can't force anyone to accept your apology. They don't owe you anything.*

I close my book and open the door to head back inside, wondering how long it'll take me to take down all these decorations.

"Hey, sorry we're late," I hear someone say behind me.

I pause in the doorway and turn back around, just in time to see Sonia dismounting from her bike, Trey's already propped up on its kickstand, and Sage removing her helmet.

"Where's Xavier?"

Sonia shakes her head. "We waited for him but he's lagging behind as usual."

And right on cue, Xavier's half-fro appears at the top of the hill.

"My bad, guys," Xavier calls out, huffing and puffing. "That hill is no joke."

Trey shakes his head, his jaw dropped. "This house is no joke. Wow."

I smile and hold open the door. "Let me give you guys the tour."

~~~

One house tour later, we're all in the living room, sprawled on the sofa, on the chairs, on the floor. I clear my throat. "So as you all probably know, I didn't ask you here just to check out this incredibly expensive house, even though that alone might've been worth the trip." My eyes move from person to person and I admit, I'm feeling a little nervous, my voice shakier than normal. "I've actually planned a group activity day, you know, if you're up for it . . ." My voice trails off, waiting for someone, anyone, to object.

Trey smiles. "I'm in, man."

And everyone, even Sonia, nods their agreement.

I can't help but grin. "Okay, then, well, let's get this day started."

11600

First on the agenda: Trey's Tour of Duty.

Trey's eyebrow rises. "Is this some sort of army game?"

I shake my head. "No, I just couldn't think of another *T* word to go with Trey that made sense. But I promise you the game is better than the name."

"Game?" Trey repeats, a twinkle in his eyes.

"Not just a game," I say, with a wink. "The best obstacle course you've ever seen."

I pull out the map I made, to show them all the obstacle course challenges.

"This is crazy," Trey says.

"It really is," Xavier agrees.

"Look at Trey," Sage says, laughing. "He's about to pass out from excitement."

"Well, then, we better get to the starting line first," I say, leading the way.

~~~

All five of us are in a horizontal line, each standing in a sack. I hand a whistle to Trey. "Since this is Trey's thing, we'll start the race on his whistle, yeah?"

"Don't even think about cheating, either," Sage says.

"I don't need to cheat to beat the four of you," Trey shoots back.

"Oh yeah?" Sonia says. "We'll see about that."

"On your mark, get set," Trey says, slipping the whistle between his lips. "Gooooo!"

The whistle sounds and we're off to the races.

The sack races, that is.

No surprise, Trey literally jumps out to a healthy lead, with Sonia right behind him. Then it's Sage, Xavier, and me.

I know I'm probably not gonna win this obstacle course, and I don't care because that's not even close to the point. I just keep hopping along, even as the distance between Trey and the rest of us increases.

Sure enough, Trey's the first person to reach the next leg of the race. The army crawl. As I hop toward the rest of the group, I watch as Trey drops onto his belly and begins crawling under the ropes and between the stakes I'd hammered into the grass. Sage, smaller than the rest of us, starts to gain ground on her big brother, and she lets him know it, too.

"Look out behind you, Trey. Winner coming through."

Sonia falls behind Xavier but stays in front of me as we snake our way through the bright green grass. "I can't believe you did all this by yourself," Xavier says as he wiggles the last of his body out from under the ropes and pops back up onto his feet.

"And we're absolutely sure these lines are secure and safe?" Sonia asks for the third time, as Sage snaps her safety vest on.

"Oh my goodness, relax, Sonia," Sage says, standing on her tiptoes and preparing to push off. "Trey's already halfway down the hill. This is a race, not a safety meeting." And with that, Sage launches herself off the hill and into the air, her now-gloved hands holding tight on to the handlebars, zipping down the corded zip line with even more speed than I'd managed the day before when I was setting it up.

"Wow, she's really moving," Sonia says, watching Sage fly down the hillside.

"Right," Xavier says. "And so am I. Deuces."

And just like that, Xavier's cruising and grooving, his head tossed back in pure joy. *"Wheeeeeeeeeeeee,"* he yells into the sky.

Sonia looks at me. "Last one down is a rotten egg," she says, knocking my handlebars out of my hands.

"Hey, that's cheating," I call after her as she zooms down the slope. "I'm gonna get you," I say as I lift my feet from the air and take off after her.

The next leg of the race would've been normally a cinch for Trey—*make ten baskets to move on*, the sign I'd written says next to the basketball court.

Except the catch is, you have to do it blindfolded. And while I thought it would at least give the rest of us a chance to make up some ground, so Trey didn't completely blow us out of the water, I never would've guessed he'd struggle as much as he does.

I also never would've guessed Xavier would be the first one done.

Sonia's next to sink her ten shots, followed by Sage.

And then it's down to me and Trey.

"Come on, Trey," Trey keeps saying to himself, as the metal box above the hoop calls out our misses and makes. *MISS*, the machine tells Trey again, and Trey says words I can't even repeat. I'm still looking for my eighth made basket when I hear Trey pick up a loose ball and launch a jump shot—*MADE*, the machine says, and Trey laughs. "Finally," he says.

By the time I run back up the hill and over to the last and final leg of the obstacle course, I know I've lost, that everyone's already taken off, cruising toward victory.

Except when I reach the front yard, everyone's still there.

I frown. "Oh, no, I say, did the batteries die? I charged them all day yesterday. I'm so sorry, guys."

But Trey shakes his head. "We were waiting for you, dude."

I shake my head. "You were? But . . . it's a race."

"Bro, we don't care who wins, we're just having a good time, and it's because of you," Xavier says.

"Yeah, so hurry up and get in your kart," Sonia says, snapping the top visor of her helmet down in place. "And let's finish this course in style."

I slide into the seat of my go-kart, and I can't stop smiling. I pull down my helmet as everyone gives each other a thumbs-up—

"On your mark," Trey shouts over the hum of the five engines. "Get set—"

But then Sage hits her gas pedal and pulls out into the street and the four of us shake our heads, before pulling out after her.

The go-kart "track" is basically a half-mile loop around two blocks and it's neck and neck for most of the race, all of us taking turns passing each other, only to be passed by the next person.

We're cruising side by side when we make the final turn for the finish line, the white ribbon fluttering in the light wind just ahead.

I zip around Xavier to claim second place behind Sage, only to have Sonia zoom around me on the other side. I glance over my shoulder to see Trey bringing up the rear, just as Xavier tries to maneuver around me. "Nice try," I yell out, and Xavier shakes his head as he's forced to fall back behind me. And it's looking like I'm headed for a third-place finish, when I realize Trey's missing. "Where did Trey go?" I try to ask Xavier but instead of answering, he uses this as an opportunity to leap ahead of me. Okay well, as long as I keep Trey behind me, wherever he is, I won't be in last, ha—

But then out of the corner of my eye, I see a blur speeding down the sidewalk—it's Trey, of course, and without anyone blocking his way, unlike the rest of us, he has a free path right to the finish line—which he happily sails through, beating Sage by a nose.

Ten minutes later, I present Trey with a brass trophy that says "Fishing Championship, Second Place," which makes Trey laugh. "Sorry, man, it was the best I could find," I explain but he just pulls me into a hug.

"Are you kidding me," he says, beaming. "It's perfect."

11700

TREY'S KEEP IT REEL

Honestly? I don't even *like* sports that much. I'm just great at all of them.

11800

"A spa day? For me?" Xavier exclaims, thoroughly confused.

"Bro, just enjoy it," Trey says, slapping Xavier on the shoulder. "Eddie's got us today."

And yeah, maybe he resisted in the beginning, but who can deny the power of a state-of-the-art massage chair—of which the Johnson family of course has FOUR, one for each of them, and today one for each of my friends.

"What about you, man?" Xavier asks, as he purrs in the chair like a happy kitten.

"I've gotta get the next thing ready," I say, lowering the light. "You guys enjoy."

Twenty minutes later, we're all sweating our butts off in the sauna.

"Wow, it's hot in here," Sonia says, wiping her forehead.

"Great for the pores," Trey assures us.

Fifteen minutes after that we're hot again, but this time it's way more bearable as we all pile into the hot tub.

"Remind me how we have all this hot water happening right now," Xavier asks.

"Johnsons are rich," I say.

"Oh yeah, right, right, I almost forgot."

Half an hour later, all of us toweled off and back to our original dry states, Xavier is all smiles. "Okay, I can't front. I did enjoy that way more than I thought. It was actually kind of dope."

I nod my head. "I'm glad you enjoyed it, but it's not over yet. There's one last thing. Follow me, please."

I lead everyone into the next room—a massive all-white bathroom that was probably the size of my family's entire house.

And in the center of it all, a special gift imported courtesy of Sally's Salon.

Xavier shakes his head. "What's that barber chair for?"

I produce a set of cordless clippers from behind my back and a handheld mirror. "I wasn't sure if you'd actually need it, but I thought I'd give you the full barbershop experience, you know?"

Xavier takes the clippers from my hand, holds them up to his face like he can hardly believe his eyes. "Is this . . . is this for real?" he asks.

"See for yourself," I say.

And I watch as he glides his thumb up the side of the chrome clippers and they twitch and hum to life—*bzzzzzzz*.

"Come on, guys," I tell Sonia, Sage, and Trey. "Let's give Xavier some privacy."

~~~

We're sliding homemade pizzas into the woodburning stove on the back patio when someone appears in the doorway, getting our attention with an extra-loud throat clear.

We all swivel around to face Xavier.

"Well, whaddya think?" he asks, slowly turning in a circle, to give us a full-360 view.

"I think . . ." I say, looking for the right words. "I think this is the fresher-than-fresh Xavier I remember."

"You look good, man," Sonia agrees. "Who would've thought a full haircut could make so much of a difference?"

Xavier laughs. "Umm, thanks? I think?" Xavier holds out his fist and I tap it with my own. "Good look, bro," he says. "This cut was almost worth all those jokes you had before."

I smile. "I'm glad, although now I guess I'll have to come up with some more material."

Xavier looks me up and down. "Yeah, you better because I still got plenty to say about you still rocking this swimsuit, bruh."

And I push him in his chest, playfully, the way you do with someone who's been your best friend since the sandbox.

"Love you, man," he says, wrapping me in a hug.

"You better," I say. "Love you, too," I add, my throat kind of burning and my eyes kind of watering from the onions on the pizzas.

11900

"Sonia's Systems?" Sonia says, reading the sign posted in the backyard. "I don't get it."

"You will," I say.

And then all five of us are zip-lining back down the hill. It's not until we make it through the garden and around the rec center (home to the indoor tennis, volleyball, and basketball courts) that Sonia finally gets it.

Which, I mean, I'd hope so, considering we're staring at the biggest outdoor movie screen I've ever seen.

"Movie night?" Sonia asks.

"Umm, maybe later," I say, producing a game controller from behind my back and tossing it to her.

She's cheesing before she even catches it.

"No waaaay, man!" She says, jumping up and down. "Are we really about to play video games on this stupid-ginormous screen?"

"Ding, ding, ding," I say, in my best game show announcer voice. "But that's not all. Let's show her what else she's won." And now I reveal the thing in my other hand and toss it over to her.

"What is it?" Sage asks.

But before I can even get out a syllable, Sonia is knocking me into the grass in a bear hug. *"Gaia's Revenge II!* This game's not even out yet! How did you do this?"

"Lucky for us they stock new movies and games for weeks before they're released. I just had to sort through a million boxes at Gamers Palace, is all."

Sonia rolls onto her knees. "I'm sorry I've been so serious this whole time."

I shake my head. "I'm sorry I don't always take things seriously enough. But you know what? I think that's why we're so tight. Because we're not just alike. Because I'm not great at the stuff you're great at, but you help me figure it out."

"And the stuff you're great at," Sonia says, smiling at me, smiling at all of us. "Like busting your butt and putting all this together, like being super thoughtful, is the kind of stuff that keeps people together for a long time."

Xavier runs his hand across the top of his fresh cut and grins. "The kind of stuff that people don't forget for even longer."

"I feel a group hug coming on," Trey says, holding out his arms.

And that's exactly what happens.

The Best Group Hug Ever Hugged by Any Group, Anywhere.

"Okay, but I have just one question," Sage says as we all finally pull apart. "Where's *my* special thing, Eddie? What about *me*?"

"Sage, c'mon," Trey says. "We were having a moment."

But I shake my head and smile. "Don't worry," I tell her. "I promise I didn't forget about you. Your thing happens after the video game tournament . . ."

12000

Pizza in our bellies, video game still buzzing in our brains, I reveal the final activity of the evening. Back on the Johnson family porch, everyone seated comfortably on the deck chairs, I stand up near the stairs and face my four friends. This time it's my turn to clear my throat.

"This is for you, Sage," I say, smiling as the sun slowly starts to set behind my back. "We've come a long way in a short time together. We've had our highs and our lows, our ups and downs. But we've always bounced back and we've always had each other's backs when it really mattered. And here's the thing I know about us . . . I know we aren't quitters. I know we are more than just survivors. Could it be random dumb luck that brought us five together? Sure. But also, what if it's not just random dumb luck? What if we're here, together, for a reason? What if we're here because all of this is meant to be? Because there's something we're supposed to do together? Either way, I believe in us. Every single one of us. Now the way I see it, there's one place that might hold the one clue that makes all these other clues make sense. That will finally lead to us getting a few answers. It's basically the one place, and not for lack of trying, we haven't quite made it to yet. And for my money, if you ask me, it's the one place we *need* to be."

"The beach!" Sage screams, jumping out of her seat and clapping her hands enthusiastically. "We're going to the beach!"

12100

"Wait," Sage says, pausing her clapping. "But how are we going to get there?"

And if my face was an emoji, it would be a shrug because, umm, I have no idea.

But I hear Real Dad chanting in my ear, *Lead, Eddie, lead.*

And so I try.

Because sometimes being a good leader means admitting when you're completely clueless.

Admitting you need help.

"I don't have even the slightest idea," I confess. "Buuuut I do know if we work together, we can definitely figure it out."

And silence falls over us as we all think hard on the next best step.

Suddenly, just as it's starting to feel a bit hopeless, Xavier snaps his fingers. "My dad has every map ever created," Xavier exclaims.

And then seeing our *really, bro* faces, he adds: "Okay, fine, yes, I'm exaggerating a little bit but seriously, dude has a lot of maps."

"It's true," Sonia confirms. "I've seen them."

"Okay, but how are a bunch of maps gonna help?" Sage wonders aloud—and I'm with her, I don't get it.

Except Xavier's already two steps ahead. "There's only one road that leads to the beach, right? And if you try to go off-road, you run into the lake on the north side or Witch Woods on the south side, yeah?"

We all mumble our agreement, still unclear where Xavier's taking us.

If only I had a map for this conversation, hehehe.

Really, Eddie?

Oh, c'mon, I had to.

"But what if that's not actually true," Xavier adds, his eyes gleaming with excitement. "What if there's another way?"

And ten minutes later, we're at Xavier's house, in his dad's office, searching for the answer to that question.

"Okay, but what exactly are we looking for, though?" Trey asks. "There's so many maps."

And he's right. Xavier's dad's office has three floor-to-ceiling bookshelves just filled with map books.

I run my fingers along their spines, reading their titles under my breath, until I find what I'm looking for.

City of Carterville, Pre–City Center Renovations.

"I don't get it," Xavier says. "What's so special about this map?"

But Sage beats me to the punch, her finger tracing a line that leads from our block all the way to the water.

"Wait, but that road doesn't exist. When they built the new highway or whatever, right?" Sonia asks, shaking her head as she studies the map again.

"Oh, it still exists all right. It's just the kind of road you're probably not sure you wanna be on, especially at night."

"Hold up," Trey says, scratching his chin. "You're talking about that old service road the farmers use for their tractors? It'll be pitch-black out there."

Sage laughs. "Dude, it's pitch-black everywhere. There's no power, remember?"

I nod, my cheeks stretching into a smile. "There's something I keep thinking about. What if we've been looking at this whole *why did everyone disappear and where are they* mystery from the wrong end?"

Xavier scratches his head, and I don't know, honestly, I sorta miss his half-fro. "Wrong end?" he asks. "What end should we be looking at?"

"We keep wondering why everyone else disappeared. But maybe that's not the right question. Maybe we should be asking ourselves, *Why are we still here?*"

Trey chews his lip. "You mean like maybe the five of us were left here for a reason?"

Sonia's eyes widen. "Wait . . . like maybe we were . . . chosen?"

Sage is grinning now. "Oooh. Chosen like we're gonna be superheroes or something."

I laugh. "I don't know about being superheroes but, yeah, maybe we're meant to do something."

"Well, if that's true," Xavier says, "seems to me we better figure out what's going on at that beach."

Trey cracks his knuckles. "You took the words outta my mouth, X. Let's do this."

Sage throws up her hands. "OMG, finally!"

And I can't help but smile, because Sage is right. Because after all we've been through, we're gonna go get the answers we all need.

Finally.

12200

Psst.

Hey.

Pssssst.

Yeah, I'm talking to you.

Hey, you wanna know the secret to not being afraid?

Okay, but fair warning, it's really gonna blow your mind.

You sure you're ready for that? To have your mind blown, which is basically equivalent to gluing a jet fuselage to the bottom of your brain and then rocket-shipping it straight to outer space, so as long as you're okay with *that*, knowing you may never see your brain again, or at the very least, that your brain will no longer work the same way it did before you knew the secret to not being afraid, then okay, I'm happy to share it with you. So as long as you know the risks, yeah?

Okay, so then, here it is.

The secret to not being afraid is . . . *drum roll, please*:

Just don't do it. Don't be afraid. And you're like, *Eddie, really, that's it? That's your big secret advice?*

Well, (1) don't knock it until you've tried it, and (2) sometimes the best advice is the most obvious advice.

But I get it, guys, so let me add one more sliver to the secret—

Don't think about how afraid you are.

Don't dwell on your fears.

Distract yourself with something, anything.

Get out of your head and get out of your own way.

12300

From the passenger seat, Sonia looks over at me and we lock eyes and she hits me with an encouraging nod, her large brown eyes filled with hope and positivity, almost as if they're whispering, *Hey, Eddie, don't worry, friend, you got this.*

Which, not gonna lie, I definitely appreciate the vote of confidence—even if it's technically not even spoken with actual words. Seriously, when you're in a car with old and new friends, getting ready to drive a car toward a location that it seems maybe you're not meant to make it to, because you're trying to figure out what happened to make your entire town suddenly disappear, umm, every ounce of optimism counts.

You know what they say: Morale matters!

Okay, maybe I've never actually heard anyone say that but, c'mon, with eight billion people on this planet, *someone* other than me had to say it at some point, right?

I mean, that's not even counting all the people who have already croaked.

I slowly press my foot deep onto the gas pedal, bracing myself in case the car suddenly lurches backward. Except we don't budge. Nothing happens. I mash my foot a little harder this time, and I can hear the engine rumbling like it's *trying* to go, but still we don't move a single inch.

"What are we waiting for?" Sonia asks. "Let's get this show on the road, cowboy."

"Yeah, let's burn some serious rubber!" Sage shouts from the back.

"It's not going," I say, confused.

Sonia reaches over and presses a button. "Parking brake was on."

I nod. "Right. Thanks. Now let's try this again, yeah?" I slide the shifter into reverse, check my rearview mirror, and—

"Wait, wait! Stop the car! We can't go yet!" Sage yells from the back seat.

12400

I stomp on the brakes, throw the car in park. "What's wrong?"

Sage grins like a cat at a one-winged bird convention and I'm thinking, *Uh-oh, now what?* "We need a name," she says.

"A name for what?" Xavier asks, who to his credit, and for the first time in the history of transportation, has not complained about being wedged in the back middle seat.

"For our group," Sage says.

"How do you mean?" Trey asks.

Sonia perks up. "Hey, you mean like the Avengers?"

Sage's face lights up. "Yep, just like the Avengers or the Fantastic Four, the Power Rangers—you know, a group nickname."

"I like that idea," I say. "But what should we call ourselves?"

Sage rubs her hands together like she's trying to start a fire—and it is in this moment that I realize this nickname thing is not coming out of nowhere. This is definitely something she's been thinking about and saving for just the right time . . .

"How about the Forever Five?"

And we all nod and shrug. "I think that works," we agree.

"The Forever Five," I repeat, as I put the car back into reverse.

"Yeah, it's definitely growing on me."

12500

We are driving toward the moon.

No, we are racing toward the moon.

Dashing to the moon.

Dashing moonward.

We are pumped.

We are ready.

We are determined.

And okay, maybe we are *also* a bit nervous, anxious, and that's fair, too—it would be completely fair to say that.

But mostly we're the first stuff I said.

12600

That's when we see the scary lights.

We see the scary lights flickering and, yo, it's wild how fast life can turn.

Like I can't even figure out how to turn on my stinking car headlights but here's life, turning on a dime, hitting a U-turn out of the blue, completely switching things up.

Maybe life has ADHD, too.

But at first I'm not sure I'm seeing what I'm seeing because it's still kinda foggy and again, no headlights for us, because I think they're broken or something, I finally found the switch thing and I flipped it but nothing happened, so—

I blink to make sure I'm not just sleepy.

Then I glance over at Sonia and her eyes are wide and her jaw has basically dropped to her lap, where it now rests atop her seat belt, so I feel like it's a safe bet to say the lights are *not* a mere figment of my imagination.

That those lights are real.

Real scary.

And I know what you're thinking, *Eddie, shouldn't you be excited that there's someone coming toward you? That there is at least one more person still around?*

I can see how you'd think that way, but honestly, all I could think inside is: What if it's aliens? Or some bad evil villain? Or a cargo truck full of snakes?

No, not like shady people. I mean, actual sssssssssssnakes.

Hey, it's like we keep saying, at this point nothing would surprise me.

All I know is those lights are getting closer and closer, which you'd expect since we're still driving in their direction. Except the rate at which they're getting closer is so much faster than if we were just driving toward them while they remained stationary.

Which means the lights are moving, too.

But not just moving.

They're moving right toward us.

"Eddie, maybe we should pull over," Xavier says. At least I think it was Xavier. I can't really be sure what happens next because my brain is too busy boxing up all its logic and reasoning, too busy packing up its common sense and don't-jump-to-conclusion-ness, too busy racing out its front door and into its own car, too busy zooming out of the city limits, leaving the *Welcome to Calm Eddieville* sign in its dust.

"Guys, I think I'm gonna be sick," Sage says.

"Are you gonna throw up?" Xavier exclaims. "Because if you throw up, I'm gonna throw up."

"Why would you throw up?" Trey asks.

"It's just what I do," Xavier says, like it's not even worth thinking about.

And I'm pretty sure Sonia and I are nodding at the same rate like, *Yep, confirmed, that's really just a thing that Xavier does in response to other people vomiting.*

And then the lights are less than a football field away.

And now I know for sure it's two lights. Two perfectly evenly spaced yellow-white lights headed up the same road we're heading down—

And now I'm wishing I hadn't insisted on taking the back road.

Now I'm wishing I'd just stayed on the main road.

Because the road we're on is almost too narrow for two cars to be on at the same time. Especially when one of the cars is being driven by someone who's only twelve and has only driven a car for however long it's been since the other day.

"Eddie, why does it seem like they're speeding up?" Sonia asks, reading my mind as usual.

"Because they are speeding up."

"Don't they see us?" Sage says.

"Quick, Eddie! Flash your lights!" Trey suggests.

"Our lights aren't working, remember?" I say.

"I knew it," Xavier groans. "We're gonna die. We're all gonna die. I knew we should've just stayed in the front yard and waited patiently, but nooooo, you guys had to insist we do this thing together. We're a group, you said, this is good for team bonding. For unity. And now the only thing we're gonna be unified in is our caskets."

"Xavier, I love you, but that's not really helpful right now," Sage says, in a weirdly calm voice.

"I think you should just stop the car and we should all jump out," Trey suggests.

"Good idea, let's do that," Xavier chimes.

"Except what if he swerves in the dark to avoid the car and veers off the road and runs us over instead?" Sonia adds.

Which is dark, definitely.

Morbid? Absolutely.

But correct? No question.

"Sonia's right," I say. "I'm gonna try to pull over—" I add, as I fumble with the switches next to the steering wheel.

In just a few seconds, I manage to activate the windshield wipers, the windshield wiper fluid, the radio, something called cruise control, and a lot of other stuff that I don't actually understand, nor was it useful.

Yep, I cycle through everything *but* the headlights.

Meanwhile the car is so close I almost have to close my eyes to avoid being blinded.

"Everyone has their seat belts on, right?" I ask, as I guide the car as far as I can to the side of the road, slowing down.

But it doesn't matter—I still can't quite get over far enough.

So the way I see it, I have two equally awful choices: I can yank the car off the road and down into the cornstalks, which seems like a surefire way to turn this story into a horror show—

Or I can hope the car charging right for us sees us at the last second and doesn't collide a hundred miles an hour into us.

I'm almost about to choose the cornfield when—

It occurs to me.

I'm wrong. I'm so happily wrong. I've never been happier to be wrong, ever.

Because I *haven't* actually tried everything!

I keep one hand firmly gripping the wheel, the car swerving a bit as the gravel and tall grass and maybe even the cornstalks on the side of the road try to pull us off-road—but with my other hand, I smash down on the center of the steering wheel and the best thing happens.

The best sound I've ever heard in my twelve years of human existence.

BEEEEEEEP!

"Ohmigod, yes, Eddie, you're a genius," Sage shouts from the back seat.

"Let's not go too crazy," Xavier says. But his tone of voice clearly says, *Thank goodness we're not gonna die, probably.*

I press the horn a few more times.

BEEP BEEEEEEP BEEEEEP.

Just to make sure.

But it doesn't seem to matter to the car. It's still headed right for us.

Judging by how fast it's going, we probably have less than ten seconds before we're all toast—

I lean into the horn, but nothing happens—the oncoming car is a missile headed for impact. And we're its target.

"Wait, why isn't it slowing down? You're blowing the horn. Doesn't it hear the horn?" Sonia says from the passenger seat, for the first time in a long time her voice not strong and confident and wise.

Her voice now like mine, shaky, quivering, afraid.

"Maybe they're listening to music?" Sage suggests.

"Or maybe it's aliens and they're gonna plow into us to destroy us?" Trey says.

Which again, poor timing.

Welp, looks like this is it.

In T-minus five seconds it'll be all over and well—

I just wanna say thank you so much for being awesome company and even better people. I really do consider you close friends now and I thank you so much for your support. We couldn't have made it this far without you. No, really, it's true. And, hey, please take care of yourself, okay? Make sure you—

Sonia reaches across the seat and grabs my hand, squeezes the crap outta my fingers, but I don't groan, I just squeeze back, and look into her eyes—

This is the last face I'll ever see on this side of life—

At least it's the face of my best friend . . . forever.

"Love you," I say.

"Love you, too," Sonia says back, quietly. "Love you all."

And then it happens—

The sharp blare of the oncoming car's horn as they see us at the last second and try to avoid us, swerving their car wildly, it fishtailing left then lurching right—

And I wait for the crunch of metal.

For the . . . afterlife? Whatever it is.

Hey, who knows, maybe we'll all teleport to wherever it is our families and friends are.

I squeeze Sonia's hand tighter and close my eyes and let the blackness settle in.

And then . . . And then . . .

12700

Nothing happens.

Somehow, by maybe an inch, the other car misses us.

How, I don't know. They must be a stunt driver or something.

Whoever that was, we owe them our lives.

But also, you'd think they'd slow down after nearing colliding with a vehicle full of kids—

Or at least brake.

But I don't even see brake lights.

All I see are the rear taillights of the car getting smaller, glowing lighter, as the car slowly disappears.

And I realize none of us have said a word. Not one.

But that part's way easier to explain than what just *didn't* happen.

Because it's hard to speak when you haven't taken a breath.

But then we all collectively breathe a deep sigh of relief. I'm pretty sure combined we sound like a hot-air balloon deflating.

And the best part about breathing is that we're all still alive.

And the other cool thing about breathing?

Is that it helps get oxygen back to your brain—and when that happens, you start thinking clearly, you see things for what they are, you develop a plan.

"You thinking what I'm thinking?" Sonia says from the passenger seat.

"Depends," I say with a devilish smile. "You thinking we should chase down that car?"

And what more can I say, except great minds think alike.

I turn the car around and floor the gas. Admittedly a little too hard because everyone falls back in their seats, like we're astronauts launching into g-force.

The other car is quite a ways ahead. If it doesn't slow down, we may lose it, because even though my driving skills are improving, guys, it's still only been a few days.

I'm far from a pro.

"We're gonna lose him," Xavier says because why bother being positive during a stressful situation.

"No, we're not," Trey says, clapping my shoulder with his long, athletic hand. Then he squeezes my shoulder for good measure. "Eddie's got this."

"No," Sage says. "Eddie's got *us*."

Except privately, internally, I'm worried that unless the other car stays going straight, we're gonna lose it. If it veers off in any other direction, there's no way we're gonna catch up to it. It could easily take two or three turns by the time we get there.

But today isn't just The Most Fun Group Day Ever, it turns out.

It's also The Group's Luckiest Day Ever, because the other car?

Stays on the same road.

And slowly but surely we start making up ground.

And not that long after, as we gain on it, decreasing the distance between its rear bumper and our front bumper, more and more I like our chances.

We got you, I think to myself. *Whoever you are . . . we got you.*

The other car bounces off the main road and now we're only five or six car lengths behind it, a comfortable distance that I do my best to maintain so that we don't spook whoever's inside. I figure, keeping a little space between us is gonna be good no matter what, in case we gotta hightail outta there, in case it's an ambush or something. *Good thing I couldn't figure out the head-light situation*, I think. Less likely to see us trailing them without headlights.

And I know what everyone in the car is thinking:

Now we're just playing monkey see, monkey do—aka the copycat game.

The Other Car turns left on Ventura Boulevard, we turn left on Ventura Boulevard.

The Other Car veers right on MLK Drive, we veer, too.

The Other Car zooms down Wilson Place, then cuts down Franklin Plaza, before knifing over to Aaron Ave—and we zoom, cut, and knife right after it.

Because (1) we happen to be awesome at the copycat game, and (2) we're just plain awesome.

And when it blows through the traffic light at Kensington Square, just barely tapping its brakes, making me wanna clench my eyes shut because what if there was another car coming from the other side street, they would've T-boned each other and that would be the end of the monkey seeing or doing.

But then I remember, oh, right, there aren't any lights working because, duh, there's no electricity and even though you'd think the Other Car Driver would've learned their lesson after nearly hitting us, that maybe there are other cars on the road that haven't figured out how to turn on their headlights, and so it's possible that being reckless could still end up in a head-on, very scary collision—

But (1) I'm assuming the driver in the Other Car cares, which is a big assumption, plus assumptions are usually dumb, if not pointless, and (2) I'm assuming the driver in the Other Car is responsible, which again, dumb, and (3) how do I know the other driver isn't just like us, like me—brand-new behind the wheel, engaging in on-the-job training, ha. In other words, cut the Other Car some slack, Eddie.

Which, fair.

And for a few moments I nearly forget I'm not alone, that my friends are in the car with me, because no one has said a word, because our words are probably trapped inside our throats, because our throats are probably clogged up with our hearts, because we nearly swallowed them back there in our near-death experience.

But then I hear someone gasp as we turn onto Ellison.

Because wait a minute, why is the car driving down *our* street?

For a second my brain gets the best of me and I start thinking, *What if Mom's in that car, how happy would I be, how hard would I hug her, even though I'm still a little teensy bit salty she grounded me from Beach Bash?*

And then this really weird thought—okay, I'm sorry, I'll try not to say *weird* anymore because yes, at this point, what *hasn't* been weird?

Okay, but this odd thought pops in my head that what if in the other car, the driver is . . . me? Like what if it is aliens taking over Carterville (for reasons I'd never understand because, um, why not Miami or Chicago or LA, although we do have a pretty awesome drawbridge here and also the downtown fountain is hella dope, too, so I kinda get it)—but yeah, what if aliens are taking over our town and they're replacing us with clones that they are controlling with surgically implanted microchips? Or what if the aliens are excellent at making disguises, like they're expert hair and makeup stylists and also killer with a sewing machine, and they're dressing up and making themselves over as each of us? What if Carterville is just the beginning of their plan to take over the entire country and eventually the world? It kinda makes sense since Ohio *is* called the Heartland, as in the heart of America, as in fairly centralized. So maybe they take us over and then slowly spread out in a circle in all directions, swapping out unsuspecting humans with alien look-alikes?

What if when the Other Car finally stops and the driver steps out, I find myself staring back at myself—ohmigod, that's gonna be so trippy! But also fun, right?!

"Earth to Eddie," a voice is saying over and over, finally snapping me from my possibly-dreamy alien takeover fantasy-nightmare situation. It's Sonia.

"Huh?" I ask. "Everything cool?"

"I said we should probably slow down because it looks like the other car is getting ready to pull into one of the driveways . . ."

"Oh, yeah, right," I say, leaning into the brake slowly, gently.

But wait, one of *these* driveways?

These are *our* driveways?

Maybe I am right. Maybe the aliens really are invading Carterville.

MY BRAIN: *Except hold up, Eddie, wouldn't they have attacked you back on the back road—dude, stop tripping.*

ME: *You right. My bad.*

MY BRAIN: *I ain't say I was right. Don't get it twisted. I just said stop tripping and I was trying to keep you chill. If you want my opinion, I'mma suggest you turn this car around and get outta Carterville immediately. Don't stop driving until you reach the ocean or something.*

ME: *Okay, (1) we don't have enough gas for that and (2) what would we do at the ocean?*

MY BRAIN: *Um, ocean stuff, duh. Build sandcastles. Take a romantic walk along the shoreline. Read a book as we inhale that warm, salty ocean breeze. I'm sure we could find some dope* *hammocks on the way, too. We could always hit up The Super*

Sports Super Store on our way outta town.

ME: *Okay, I'm shutting you down now, that's enough, thanks.*

"Are you okay, Eddie?" Xavier whispers as I park the car six or seven houses away, all five pairs of our eyes locked onto the Other Car as it slowly pulls to a stop in front of a house. In front of . . .

12800

What in the world?

"We're not gonna get a good look at them from here," Sonia says.

"Maybe we should get out of the car and creep up from the other side of the street," Trey says.

Wait, did I miss something? Where did the person/alien/driver go? They've disappeared.

And then KNOCK KNOCK—

Someone taps on the glass and I'm pretty sure that I just proved, in case you were wondering, that it is indeed possible to have a heart attack at age twelve.

Also, I may or may not have yelped.

And okay, I may or may not have also jumped and smacked my head on the roof.

"Dude, hurry up, before we lose them," Xavier says, opening my car door for me.

And I realize I'm in the car alone.

"Where's everyone else at?" I ask.

"They're following the driver," Xavier answers.

"Following the driver where?"

"How am I supposed to know? I hung back to get you. Let's catch up to the others."

And we do. Except for Sonia. She's still missing. Where is she? Talk about a bad time for a potty break.

"Wait, they went inside my house?" I ask Trey.

He nods. "And Sonia followed them in, too."

My eyes probably get as wide as saucers. "You kidding me? Alone?"

Trey nods. "I'm guarding the front door and Xavier is gonna go around to the back door. You should probably use the—"

But then there's a loud scream inside the house, and it sounds like Sonia, and I don't stick around for Trey to finish his sentence. I race through the front door and into the house. "Sonia, are you okay?! Where are you?! Look, alien Eddie, I don't know who you think you are but we're onto your world domination plan and I'm sorry, but it's not gonna happen. Actually, sorry not sorry, ha!"

Except I don't see or hear anything on the first floor.

Partly because it's late at night now and without power, it's spooky black.

I remember the flashlight in my pocket and pull it out, snapping the rubber power button on. But nothing happens. I press it again and still nothing. Great. No light. Well, this isn't super, heart-wrenchingly scary. Except there's no time to waste being indecisive or scared. Not when Sonia, my best friend, might be in trouble.

I sprint up the stairs and now I'm in the long second-floor hallway.

I stop to listen for signs of life and that's when I see it, the quick flicker of a light at the far end of the hall. I creep slowly down the hall, tiptoeing my way, my hand just lightly grazing the wall so I keep my bearings and don't trip and fall.

I hear a noise behind me and whirl around just in time to see three creatures charging me. And I don't mean to do it but I can't help it, I can't stop myself, it's just instincts and who can control those, you know, it's not my fault I—

I scream.

Which makes the creatures scream, which makes me scream even louder, and also maybe jump excitedly into the air at least half a dozen times, jumping in the air the same way you would if your friend called to tell you they got two tickets to see your favorite band's concert tonight. Except I'm . . . you know . . . not excited or elated, and so I keep screaming before finally turning away, abruptly ending my trampoline act. And now I'm screaming as I'm running away, headed right at the original light I saw only seconds ago, because to be real, I completely forgot about it seeing how currently my brain's buzzing with only one thought—

MY BRAIN: *See, now we about to die. We should be scooping up those hammocks and feeling the warm ocean mist spritzing across our faces but you had to be a hero. You had to be—*

Except the three creatures turn out to be:

"Bro, relax, it's just us," Xavier says. And although I can only barely make out his face, I don't need to see him to know he's giving me that patented *are you outta your mind* Xavier look.

Which, my answer is: probably.

And then I realize where we are.

We're just outside the one door I never ever stand near.

The one room that I am utterly and completely banned from entering—

And I hear rustling inside and I think, *Sonia*. Sonia is inside the room, but then something taps my shoulder and I whirl around and—

"Ohmigod, did you guys hear me scream? I walked right into a spiderweb. I'm so sorry. I couldn't help it. It was totally instinct. But hey, I still followed the driver, although admittedly I was so distracted by the spider situation that I didn't keep up with them, so they could be anywhere in the house, waiting to leap out and ambush us and—"

But Sonia never finishes her sentence.

12900

Because that's when the forbidden door swings open swiftly, as if it was forced open by a cannon, and the driver, a large hulking shadowy thing, stands there, ready to eat us, or do weird experiments on us—okay, I'm sorry, I won't say *weird* anymore, sheesh. I'm only human, guys.

And I'm so close to the driver creature that I can smell them. I can feel their hot breath beaming down on my face. And it's like I can't move. Like they've used their advanced mental abilities to freeze me or paralyze me or something.

And then there's only bright white light, as its hand or leg or whatever its appendages are called thrusts its eye-blinding palm-light in my eyes.

"I should've known it was you idiots," the Driver says.

"Wait," I say, the words catching in my throat. "Is that . . ."

The light pulls back.

And my worst fears are confirmed.

It's . . .

"The Bronster! What are you doing here?" I ask.

And everyone else starts assaulting The Bronster, except not physically but with questions, like:

Where have you been?

Where is everyone?

Have you seen anyone else?

On and on and on—until finally The Bronster holds his hands up and swipes them violently in the air. "Enough," he barks. "Shut up! All of you!"

And we do shut up, not because we're scared, though—okay, it's important you know that, that we're only shutting up so we can hear his answers to all our questions.

"Now I've got one question for you, Eddie, and you better think long and hard before you answer it or you're dead, you hear me?" The Bronster says, his nostrils flaring, his long meaty finger jabbing me in my chest.

I gulp harder than I mean to and my throat burns.

And then he says it, the words roaring out of his mouth in a rampage—

"HAVE YOU BEEN IN MY ROOM?!!!??!!?!"

An extremely brief closing note from our storytelling master, Eddie Gordon Holloway, who just hooked you all the way, again, mostly, kind of, sort of:

Okay, so there you have it. Another episode in the Forever Five saga. And I know, I know, we still haven't quite made it to the beach. Trust me, no one's more disappointed than me—except maybe Sage.

But look at the bright side: This time we were closer than ever. Annnnd nothing horrible happened to us along the way, which is a pretty big deal—you know, unless you count finding out that The Bronster is still alive and well, ugh.

Anyway, thank you, guys, for sticking with us again. We've definitely been through a lot—not just the five of us—but you, too.

Seriously, we couldn't have done any of this without you.

And even if we could, I wouldn't want to.

So, yeah, until next time, this is your friend Eddie Gordon Holloway, signing off—

And while we work on a way to make it to the beach, why don't you treat yourself to a human ice cream sundae on me. I think you know where you can find a pretty awesome recipe, haha!

PEACE!*

---

*Hopefully.

ACKNOWLEDGMENTS

Thank you to the perfect editor for this book—Maya, I couldn't have done this without you and I wouldn't wanna try. Thank you for your grace, humor, and keen eye.

Shout-out to Matt, for trusting me to finish what we started.

Thank you to Beth for always believing and being the best agent at agenting.

Thank you to my incomparable family: Brooklyn, Kennedy, Allie, Grey, Mom, and Dad. I love you, eternally.

Thank you to my found family: James, Ashley, Caron, Dennis, Leah, Drew, Becky, Alex, Jen, Natasha, Christina, Meredith, Bri, Emily, and Jerry. You are my people.

Thank you, Hannah, for backing me up.

Thank you to all the amazing people at Scholastic who helped make this book a reality; you rock!

Thank you to every librarian and public library that let me hang out during their normal business hours, no questions asked. Please, please support your local public library!

Thank you to every industrious, hardworking bookseller, but especially Mac's Backs for championing my work and supporting local authors and our community. Please, please support your local indie booksellers!

And thank you to every kid who thinks I'm "kinda funny": I understand your hesitation to just say "funny" and I still thank you for your kinda support.

And to everyone's who's ever had to walk/run/somersault urgently while in flip-flops, you're a real one. Respect.

ABOUT THE AUTHOR

justin a. reynolds has always wanted to be a writer. *Opposite of Always*, his debut novel, was an Indies Introduce selection and a *School Library Journal* Best Book, has been translated into seventeen languages, and is being developed for film with Paramount Players. He hangs out in Northeast Ohio with his family and likes it, and is probably somewhere, right now, dancing terribly. His second novel, *Early Departures*, published September 2020, and his third novel, *Miles Morales: Shock Waves*, published June 2021. You can find him at justinareynolds.com.